Written by
Julia Hall

Published in association with
Bear With Us Productions

© **2021 Julia Hall**
Magic and Me

Illustrated by Leanne Allen
Cover by Richie Evans
Graphic design by Luisa Moschetti

www.justbearwithus.com

Illustrated by
Leanne Allen

Written by
Julia Hall

Chapter 1

Prince Austin is dead!

The news ripples throughout the city like a stone splashing in the pond, the castle in the centre, cascading down past the rich mansions, through the markets to arrive at our poverty stricken village.

My sister and I live here in our small hut that we call home, built mostly from mud and stone. It's just one room with a fire that we use to cook on, keeping us mostly warm and dry. Our parents died last year while they were delivering goods for the local farmer. Their cart turned over after the horse saw a snake and bolted. We had to give the farmer almost all the money we had towards his damaged goods that had fallen in the river.

You would think that my sister, Caroline and I would get along as there is just the two of us but we don't. We rarely speak to each other. Caroline only talks to me in small grunted commands, as if she's weighed down with the responsibility of looking after us both.

"The prince was murdered," she states to me as she stirs the stew cooking on the fire. I stare at her; my mouth open wide. We despise the royals, but they are the foundation of our lives. The prince was the only heir, without him there is no one to carry on the line. This has never happened before, not in the thousand years that our island kingdom was created.

"How?" I ask in a whisper.

"I'm not sure, some are saying that he was stabbed in the back whilst out in the courtyard, others are saying he was pushed from the castle roof," she replies not looking at me, her concentration still on the stew. I collect the bowls and spoons and set them on the table, my mind in a daze.

"Was there nothing that could be done?" I ask hesitantly. Caroline suddenly pauses from stirring the stew, her shoulders tense.

"No, there was no magic that could cure him," her voice breaks roughly in her reply. The subject of magic is very rarely spoken about between us. Most people in the kingdom have some magic within them. The royals use it all the time - it is fun and games to them.

The rich families in their mansions use it to do little jobs to make life easy and carefree, or to punish their servants. The rest of the kingdom are forbidden. It's only to be used by those with wealth and privilege. I have seen some families in the houses around me use it, maybe to quickly light a fire or to make a burden lighter. I pretend not to see, for knowing is dangerous. What is more frustrating for us is that neither Caroline or I have any magic at all.

Our mum had magical ability, she could make plants grow quickly, vegetables would grow faster and fruits blossom on the trees. This helped our starving tummies on many occasions. Our dad had a little magic but whenever he tried to use it something would usually go wrong - sparks would fly around the room catching the beds on fire. I smile to myself in amusement at the memory.

"Amelia!" Caroline shouts at me. By the thunderous look on her face, this isn't the first time she has called my name. Shaking my head erasing the memories of my parents I pass the bowl over into her outstretched hand. She puts a small amount of stew in it, barely enough to cover the base and hands it back to me.

"What do you think the royals will do now?" I ask her as I hand over her bowl to fill. She stops and looks at me. Our features are very similar, with our heart-shaped faces and dimples that only appear when we laugh. Her hair is a little darker brown than mine but much shorter. Her's reaches her chin, while mine hangs in long waves down my back. Being three years older than me, at fifteen, her appearance shows more maturity and hardship than mine.

"I have no idea, but knowing the royals, it will not be good!" She states. We eat our meagre stew in silence as usual, rinse the bowls and then get into the bed together fully clothed. I watch the glowing embers of the fire dwindle, thinking about our conversation and realise that it is the most we have spoken in months.

The next morning, I head out to the fields to help the farmers with the lambing. I have various jobs but this is my favourite. The days are long and tiring but I enjoy working with the animals and the farmers are friendly as long as you work hard. This is my first day back this year having worked with the blacksmith for most of the winter. The blacksmith is a cruel man, if you don't keep up the pace, he will strike you without a second thought but his hot shack keeps out the fierce winds and icy cold rain. We desperately need his money, so I'm grateful for the job.

Caroline works at a factory making clothes for the rich. She works with silk and lace, nothing like I have ever seen before. The twelve hour days are hard but the work is year-round, so it is a steady income.

The sun is rising over the hills, making the frost on the grass shimmer, the wetness soaking my shoes and freezing my feet. I shiver in my thin cardigan, long tunic and loose trousers, my outfit is a mix of my mum and dad's old clothes. The trousers are too long - my dad was a tall man so I roll them up as best I can but they drag in the grass. The tunic was my mums and billows out over my slight frame.

It doesn't take me long to get to the barn where the sheep are all compactly penned. The strong smell of straw and manure hits my nose and I wince at its odour, my face screwing up and my eyes watering. There are three others here and the eldest, Tom has already grabbed a sheep and has it pinned to the ground to help with its delivery. He is fifteen, three years older than the two girls that are with him, Jessica and Alice who are the same age as me.

"Morning!" I shout, trying to be heard over the noise of the sheep.

Alice turns towards me and smiles. She has grown a lot in the past year, making her a few inches taller than me. Her blond hair is in a long plait down her back and her green eyes sparkle in delight. She has a large family, being the youngest of six siblings and finding work for all of them can be very difficult. Last year we became very close when I found her in the shed crying as she didn't have another job to go to over the winter.

"Morning!" She shouts back and bounds over towards me. Jessica gives me a small nod but briskly turns back to the sheep. Her sharp eyes scanning for any that seem to be ready to give birth.

"How are you?" I ask Alice quietly. Although starvation and horror are all around us, no one talks about it openly, everyone seeing it as a failure if we can't afford the things we need.

"I'm OK, I managed to get a few odd jobs that kept us going but I'm glad to be back here. How are you? Was the blacksmith awful again?" She looks at me worriedly. Trying not to wince in pain with the latest bruise still swollen on my shoulder, I determinedly put a happy smile on my face.

"It was the usual," I sigh and leave it at that. Alice grabs my hand as we hurry to join the others, we don't want to be caught talking; this job is worth too much to both of us.

The morning is hard and laborious, I manage to help deliver the babies of three sheep, one of them having twins. One, however, delivers a stillborn and no matter what I do to coax it, the lamb doesn't survive. This is never good news, without a healthy lamb the childless sheep's fate is uncertain.

I look at the dead lamb laying on the straw. The mother tries to lick it clean, her instincts telling her to do it. Suddenly she looks at me straight in the eyes. She looks sad and scared as though she knows that there is no hope for her baby or herself. I gently pat her on the head.

"It will be OK, don't worry," I tell her. She gives me a loud 'Baa' as though she has understood and turns around, leaving the lifeless baby on the floor for me to dispose of.

Alice and I get to take our lunchtime together, so we head to the main building. Inside it is packed with workers, usually, it is fairly quiet but as we head to get our ration of porridge there seems to be only one conversation buzzing around - that of the dead prince.

"It is rather awful," Alice says suddenly as we sit down. Scraping a small spoonful of porridge out of my bowl I savour its stickiness in my mouth. The news of the prince has shocked everyone here and they are busy gossiping about how it will affect the kingdom.

"Yes, it's terrible. I wonder what the royals will do now with no heir? The Queen is far too old to try for another. Do you think they will find some long-distance relative?" I ask.

Alice merely shrugs as she puts a heaped spoonful in her mouth and chews. I try and listen to the conversations around us for their opinions but they all seem as clueless as us, with some wild ideas scattered around.

"I'll be the next heir, come and get me! I'll even marry a princess for you!" One boy nearby shouts, his table all laugh at his suggestion no doubt all dreaming of being whisked away to the castle where only fine clothes and mountains of food await.

"Wouldn't that be a dream come true?" Alice says, her eyes glazed as she imagines how her life would change in an instant.

"I'm not sure I would get on with the royals, no matter how full my tummy is," I state as I finish my last mouthful. "Come on, or we'll be late," I say pulling her up from the chair as we hurry back to the barn.

The rest of the day goes by uneventfully. Only a few more sheep deliver their babies, so we keep ourselves busy cleaning out the pens, feeding and doing odd jobs. There is little time to speculate more about the dead prince.

Alice and I walk home together as the sun begins to fade. I need to hurry to get some rice from the market but Alice is in no rush.

"If I get home too early then I will have to cook," she complains as I urge her forward. I give a big sigh and roll my eyes.

"If I don't hurry then there won't be anything to cook!" I exclaim. I could leave her and go by myself but it is nice to have her friendship. All that awaits me at home is a brooding Caroline and a quiet house. Reluctantly I slow down, faster than Alice would've liked but at a pace where I won't be getting to the market too late.

"My sister Lucy is getting married to Vincent, the baker's son," Alice says quietly. I know that she is close to her sister and the loss of income will affect the household greatly. Lucy works at the same factory as Caroline but works in the office ordering materials.

"Congratulations, that's a good match," I reply, smiling. Suddenly Alice stops and looks around hesitantly.

"Vincent isn't very nice at all but he's been pursuing Lucy for ages and she's been pushing him away. Then one day he saw her use...She did..." Alice stutters. My heart pounds as I realise what Alice means. Vincent must have seen Lucy do magic and now must be blackmailing her to marry him. I have seen many deals take place when someone has been found out. If someone reports you to the royals then you are taken and never seen again.

"Oh," I say looking around also. "Why was she doing...?"

"She wouldn't say," Alice answers looking down awkwardly. We walk some more in silence. I don't know what to say. If Vincent is truly awful, then I feel very sorry for Lucy but she shouldn't have taken the risk of being seen. If I had magic, then I doubt I would use it unless in an emergency; it just isn't worth it.

"I'm sure she will be OK," I say weakly, unsure of my own words. Alice nods.

"Have you...?" She blurts out and looks at me, her eyes wide open in fear.

"No, I don't have any," I say shaking my head. "Mum and dad did, Caroline and I don't," I reply uneasily. To talk of magic is just as bad as showing it in my opinion but I trust Alice and it's nice to have a friend. I look at her expectantly, wondering for the first time if she does.

"I do," she mouths, not daring to say it out loud. For a moment I'm instantly jealous. To have that power, to be able to do something extraordinary must feel amazing but to have that fear, of always being caught, to always be looking over your shoulder must be difficult to live with.

"What can you do?" I ask curiously. Alice looks around once again and pulls my arm, so I stop. She then gets closer to me, so close we could almost be hugging. Between us she holds out her right hand and there, her fingertips are glowing blue, lighting up the space between us.

"Wow," I gasp as I step back. Alice quickly smothers the lights and looks fearful once again. "I won't tell anyone, I promise. I was just a bit shocked. Thank you though... for trusting me," I say flustered.

Later, after I have said goodbye to Alice and head towards the market, I wonder what magic must feel like and if I would have trusted her enough to show her my secret. It is only after I buy my rice and start heading home that my thoughts are interrupted by two soldiers heading towards me. Putting my head down, I try not to look guilty, Alice's secret is now mine and I must try and keep it no matter what. As they get closer, I hold my breath anxiously.

"We are rounding them up tomorrow," one guard utters to the other as they brush past me. I glance at their backs as they stride on, taking no notice of me at all. A bad feeling washes over me as I think about their words. Who or what is being rounded up tomorrow?

It is only when I am safely back at home that my heart stops pounding. I light the fire, boil the water, take out a few wilted and wrinkled vegetables and start chopping them up to put with the rice. All the time wondering what the soldiers meant.

Caroline comes in just as the meal is nearly ready. It is her turn to set the table as I fill the bowls with rice. We start eating in our usual silence until I can't keep quiet anymore.

"I heard some soldiers talking in the village, they were saying they were going to round them all up tomorrow. What do you think it means?" I ask worriedly. Caroline looks at me and sighs, I get the feeling that she was hoping for another day of silence.

"It could mean anything, stop worrying about it," she says frustratedly. We continue eating and when I've finished, I wash up and we both do our usual routine. That night I toss and turn, a feeling of foreboding creeping along my skin.

Chapter 2

The next day I am on edge as I do my work and barely say anything to Alice all morning. She keeps giving me fearful glances, probably thinking that it is her secret that is worrying me. I don't know why I can't shake the feeling off that something is about to happen but it stays with me. At lunch, I am about to tell Alice everything as we leave together, but that is when I see them. The farm is surrounded by soldiers.

"You told Amelia! How could you?" Alice screams at me as the soldier's come up to her and grab her arms. She kicks and screams, tears falling from her eyes as they pull her away. Frozen, I just stand there confused; I didn't tell! I want to shout but my mind and body won't move as I watch her get taken away. I get startled out of my trance and start to scream as someone grabs me from behind, arms wrapping around me holding me tightly.

"Help! Help!" I cry out frantically searching for anyone that can save me but all I can see are soldiers carrying children. Some are over soldier's shoulders, others are kicking and screaming like Alice. Numbly I stop struggling, the arms around me are strong and it's useless to try to escape, they are only hurting me as they dig into my flesh. The soldier seeing my obedience takes me roughly by the arm as he marches me to the other side of the field.

There waiting for us are two trucks side by side. I have never seen one up close before and feel apprehensive as the soldier pushes me into the back. Inside it's dark as the windows are covered. There are three other children huddled in the back. I recognise Tom across from me. His eye is bruised and it looks like it's starting to swell, he must have put up a fight. The other two boys both beside him I don't know other than passing or in the meal hall.

The engine starts up and a soldier gets in beside me. I can feel the vibrations right through my body and a lurch in my stomach as the truck begins to move. We are all quiet as we drive out of the field. I look at each of the others individually. I have never seen Tom use magic, or even have suspicions he has the ability. The other two I don't know at all, but one thing is very clear, they have got the wrong person in me. Studying the guard by my side I notice he is quite old, probably thirties with stubble grazing his chin. He is wearing the usual soldier outfit of grey and black with a baton strapped to his side. He has taken his helmet off and it is resting on his lap. He must feel confident that we aren't going to be any trouble. I feel the need to tell him that I am innocent, that I can't do magic but I know that he won't care. I have seen and heard the same pleas as men, woman and children have been taken and dragged away, just like I have been now. My eyes begin to water as I wonder what awaits us all when this truck stops.

We drive for a long time. We seem to be going uphill for a lot of the journey and that can only mean one thing - we are headed for the castle. Anxiously I wait for the truck to stop and the doors to open - for our fates to be revealed. I should be scared right now but I'm numb with shock. The others' have the same looks on their faces. Suddenly the soldier starts fidgeting and puts his helmet on. We must be close, I look at Tom and see the panic in his one eye, the other is now swollen closed. The truck stops and the soldier steps out.

"Everyone out now!" He commands.

Together, Tom and I get out first. The sunlight blinds my eyes at the sudden change of light, but I see that the sun is starting to disappear over the horizon. Looking around there are five other trucks, children spilling out of them all looking battered and bruised. Alice comes out of one furthest from me and our eyes lock. Her swollen, red eyes look shocked to see me here. She knows that I can't do magic, so why have I been taken? In front of us is a large stone building, behind I can glimpse parts of the castle.

"Everyone line up!" Another soldier commands, so we all meekly form a line. Alice is near the front and I am near the middle with Tom behind me. There are about twenty of us all in a row, girls and boys of around my age to Tom's. With the soldiers surrounding us, we all walk into the building quietly.

If anyone expected the building we enter to be full of the

splendour we imagined, then they would be very disappointed. All that is before us is a large high-ceilinged room with two long wooden tables. There's a raised platform at the far end and standing on it is a severe-looking woman. Her black hair is tightly in a bun and her black skirt with white blouse is clean and unwrinkled.

"Sit down!" She shouts, her voice echoing in the near-empty room. Looking up ahead I see that Alice sits at the left table. Hurrying forward, nearly pushing a boy over in my haste, I manage to sit opposite her. She glances at me distrustfully and then stares at the woman before us. I desperately want to tell her that I didn't tell anyone her secret but no one is talking, all that can be heard is the creaking of chairs and the shuffling of feet. When it is quiet the woman clears her throat and begins to speak.

"My name is Mrs Steerly. I am sure that you have all heard about the prince's untimely death which has left us all without a royal line. One of you here will take his place. Don't think for a second that you can measure up with the greatness of Prince Austin! He was a magnificent prince and next to him you look like the village rats that you are! However, you are the only available solution. Whilst you are here, you will train, learning how to use your magic and act accordingly as royalty should. It is not going to be easy and punishments will be given for underachieving. You don't have any options other than to succeed."

Panicking, I look around the room. I need to tell them that I don't have any magical ability - but what will happen to me? Will they just send me home, back to Caroline and the farm or do something else? Not everyone has magic, surely there are some here like me that don't have any?

Alice looks at me with pity, no matter what we've had to endure so far at least she is secure in the knowledge she has magic. Just as I gather the courage to raise my hand telling them of the mistake Mrs Steerly starts talking again.

"Firstly, there is a great deal about magic that only the royalty or their household know, for example, that there are four different types of magic. Earth, Fire, Water and Air. You will all be put into the correct groups and learn in those groups. Secondly, all royalty has a magical creature that is bonded and trained to be their aid in their magic. It will become your companion and will protect you from harm. Prince Austin's was a dragon, which has now been put to death for its failure. Lastly, if you don't become the heir your creature will be taken away and you will work as a servant for the royal house for the rest of your miserable lives or you will be killed."

Gasps are heard around me as I look around the room, panic in the eyes of everyone I see. How can I own up to not having magic now? They have told me secrets only royalty know - I will be killed for sure! Somehow, I'm going to have to escape before they realise. Somehow, I'm going to have to pretend before I'm found out!

I'm too busy panicking to realise what is happening around me but suddenly, there is a plate of food in front of me. Slices of ham, potatoes and carrots are piled high on my plate. Back in the village there was never enough to eat so even though I feel sick with worry, I can't resist the food on the table. Picking up the fork, I start eating slowly. The ham is delicious, much better meat than I have ever tasted before, the potatoes have a crisp skin and the carrots have been coated in honey. The room around me is still silent, all of us concentrating on our food, processing what we've been told and too scared to speak.

After all of us are finished the royal servants come and clear away our plates. They are dressed in brown tunics and trousers, most of them are skinny and look exhausted. With a sinking feeling, I realise this could easily be my fate by tomorrow.

The soldiers usher us all out of a side door and down a long corridor. There is nothing on the walls, just plain grey stone with electric lights on the ceilings. Electricity still fascinates me; it is not something that our village sees much of. Just the lights of the rich and royalty far in the distance from where I live, mingling with the stars in the sky.

We come to a stop with two doors in front of us.

"Boys in the right door, girls to the left," one of the soldier's says and then waits for us all to enter, the door is then shut behind us with a loud slam. The large room is full of beds, each with some pyjamas on top and by the looks of it, another outfit. I go to the bed in the corner and sit on it heavily. Alice takes the bed next to me.

"What are you going to do?" She asks me quietly. All the other girls are busy putting on their nightclothes, some are talking, other's look like they are doing everything automatically. None are looking our way.

"Escape I guess," I reply, my heart beating madly with anxiety.

We both get ready for bed and I slip under the covers. It feels strange to be in a bed by myself. Normally Caroline would be next to me moaning that my feet were cold or stealing the covers. I wonder what she is thinking right now. Does she know that I was snatched away from work? Surely the village is talking about it. Is she missing me, or is worried?

We didn't have the best relationship but she is still my sister. She is the only family I have left.

Chapter 3

It takes me a long time to get to sleep, but I must do, as when I open my eyes again the girls are hastily putting on the clothes we found and a soldier is waiting at the door.

We are all taken back to the large hall for breakfast which is porridge with honey. Even though one of us will be the new heir, it seems we won't be getting as lavish food as some of us had dreamed. All that can be heard is a few whispers but mostly everyone keeps quiet. Alice gives me a few furtive glances but I can't meet her eyes, I don't know how long I can keep the secret of not having any magic for and her nervousness is making my anxiety worse.

Just as we all finish Mrs Steerly enters the hall in another crisp outfit. Everyone sits up straighter and the room goes deathly quiet. No one wants to upset her and be punished.

"Come with me," she commands. Chairs can be heard scraping the rough ground as we all do as we are told.

We walk a different way down the corridor this time, the only things we see are closed doors as we pass. Abruptly the line ahead of me stops and I glimpse Mrs Steerly's arm unlock a door to the right. We all file inside obediently.

The first thing I notice is the incredible heat that smacks

me in the face and slithers down my body as I enter. The room is humid with a fine mist that seems to coat my skin. To the right, there are benches that some of the children are starting to sit on. To the left, the mist is thicker and I am confused to see what appears to be round rocks evenly spaced in rows. Alice sits beside me on the bench. When we are all seated, Mrs Steerly picks up a notepad and stands in front of us, the mysterious stones behind her.

"When I point to you, you will tell me your name and your age. You will then place your hand on each of the eggs, starting from left to right until one lights up, if none respond in the first row you will carry on to the second and so forth. When it lights up, you will pick it up and take it to your seat. Is that clear?" She instructs matter of factly.

The stones are eggs? I have no idea what's going on but children around me are all nodding. Looking at Alice, she thankfully seems as confused as I am.

"You!" Mrs Steerly points at a boy a few years older than me. He rises to his feet, his eyes shining in fear.

"My name is Peter, and I am fourteen," he states and then gingerly walks over to the first stone/egg. Nothing happens when he touches the first row, nor the second. Feeling the tension swell in the room I hold my breath as we wait. Peter shifts nervously from egg to egg and gives Mrs Steerly unsure glances, but she doesn't respond, merely looking on with vague interest. Finally, on the third row Peter touches one of the eggs and a blazing light fills the room. I squint my eyes at the sudden brightness, some of the other children holding out their hands or arms in front of their faces, protecting their eyes. Peter grasps his egg and sits back down on the end of the bench looking relieved. Curiously looking at the egg, I notice it is about the size of a small melon with a rough surface.

"You!" Mrs Steerly says again, pointing to another child, a girl this time.

"My name is Mia, and I am twelve," she says in a timid voice. She goes over to the eggs hesitantly but we are all surprised when the second egg she touches glows brightly. She sits down, a smile on her face. I only glance at her egg, which is similar to the first but seems to have swirls of white ingrained into it.

Mrs Steerly carries on down the line of children and we all watch with interest at how long it takes for an egg to glow. My anxiety grows as more children collect their eggs and when I'm not feeling at all ready, she points to me.

"Amelia, aged twelve," I say loudly, my voice shaking with nerves. Reaching the first egg, I hesitantly touch it. The surface is as rough as it looks but also feels delicate, not as hard and solid as I would have expected. As I carry on down the line my heart beats harder and faster. What if none of them glows? Will they realise that I have no magic? Getting to the fifth row I can feel sweat trickling down my skin, the mist getting heavier the further back I go. Tears begin to mix with the wetness on my face as I realise there are only three eggs left. I am just about to accept that my fears have come true, that they will see I am not supposed to be here when suddenly the light from the egg I am touching dazzles my eyes. Blinking rapidly to clear my vision I grasp the egg and head back to the bench in a daze. Alice looks at me worriedly and then stands up. It is now her turn.

I am torn between watching Alice and studying my egg more closely. I don't have to wait long though as the familiar blinding light fills the room and I feel the bench bump as Alice sits down next to me. She is beaming, her arms wrapped protectively around her egg. Relieved, I smile back at her.

Suddenly all around us, the other children gasp, whilst I had been looking at Alice, I had not been paying attention. I look forward quickly. There, standing at the very back, near to where I had picked up my egg, is a tall boy and he has turned around to face us. Realisation dawns on me; he has done what I was so afraid I was going to do. He has touched all of the eggs and none have glowed. Mrs Steerly's lips are pursed and a deep frown is etched into her skin, revealing the wrinkles around her forehead and eyes.

"Come here!" She commands her voice as stern as her appearance. The boy walks over and stands before her. Before I can even blink, Mrs Steerly's arm draws back and her hand slaps the boy around the face. The boys head jerks to the side, his body following as he falls heavily to the floor.

"GET OUT!" She shouts, her voice echoing around the room.

As fast as he can the boy scrambles up on to his hands and

knees, before he is even upright, he runs out of the door. Briefly, I see a soldier grab hold of him roughly as he is taken down the corridor. I look again at Mrs Steerly. I realise my mouth is open wide with shock so I close it quickly, my teeth tapping together with a loud click. She takes a deep breath, releasing it slowly and rubs her palms down her skirt as though she's trying to wipe them clean. She then points to the next child in the row and we all continue, just as though nothing has happened.

Chapter 4

It doesn't take much longer for all of us to be sitting on the bench clutching our eggs. Looking around the other shocked faces, I also realise that all the eggs are similar except they each have either white, red, green or blue swirls. Puzzled, I look at Alice's, both of ours have swirls of blue. Before I can really give it much thought, Mrs Steerly stands in front of us once again.

"Come in please tutors," she shouts. Three men and one woman enter the room. They're as smartly dressed as Mrs Steerly except the other woman doesn't look quite as stern, her brown hair is loose around her shoulders. One of the men looks at us and wrinkles his nose, appearing to have smelt something unpleasant.

"When I call your name, you will stand, take your eggs and follow your appointed tutor. Andrew, Olivia, Robert, Sarah and Ian you will be with Mr Majors," Mrs Steerly instructs.

The five children cautiously get up and follow the wrinkled-nosed man. I watch them go, relieved that I am not in his group. Mrs Steerly then clears her throat, so we all focus our attention on her once again.

"Mia, Laura, Ben, Claire and Liam will be with Mr Shielding," she instructs. The tutor, who has a short grey beard with bright blue eyes that are shining behind thick glasses, gestures for the children to follow him.

As they leave the room, I clutch hold of Alice's arm, scared that we will be parted from one another. She responds by giving my arm a tight squeeze. There's only one man and one woman left; I look at each of them in turn. The man stands calmly with a blank expression, the woman is watching Mrs Steerly nervously, her hands clasped in front of her firmly.

"Alice, Damian, James and Amelia you will be with Miss Clover," Mrs Steerly instructs. Sighing with relief, I clutch my egg to my chest as I follow Alice out of the door, the boys following behind us. Miss Clover briskly walks in front of us, her heeled shoes tapping against the stone floor. We all try to keep up as best we can without dropping the eggs we are all holding.

"Come along now, there's much to be sorted," Miss Clover says in a sing-song tone. We follow her through corridor after corridor and up some winding steps and then through another corridor. This place is a maze, I think as I become confused and disorientated. We pass by an open door and I see some of the other children and their tutor.

Finally, Miss Clover stops and opens a large wooden door. Inside there are six beds, three on either side. By each bed, there is a small cupboard and at the foot, there is some sort of nest made of feathers. A curtain can be pulled around the beds for privacy. In front of a large bay window, there's a large tank of water with a few large rocks in it. I look at the items with confusion. Alice walks over to the tank and peers intently inside. Miss Clover walks into the room and stands with her hands grasped once again.

"This is where you will all sleep from now on, you can each pick a bed," she says. "The nests are for your eggs. Please keep the eggs on the nests as much as possible, the feathers are phoenix's so will keep the eggs nice and warm. I will give you a few minutes to settle in. I will be waiting outside."

As soon as Miss Clover has left, one of the boy's rushes to the furthest bed and jumps on it, nearly dropping his egg.

"This bed is mine!" He announces. He is tall and bulky looking, nothing like the half-starved slight frames of the rest of us. This boy doesn't look like he has seen that much hardship in his life. He is probably about fourteen or fifteen with piercing green eyes and light brown hair which falls over his eyes, he keeps sweeping it out the way with his hand. I wonder what part of the village he was from; did they grab him and force him into a truck like the rest of us?

Alice and I go to the other side, both wanting to put as much distance from him as we can. Putting my egg down on the nest I slowly sit on the bed, feeling its softness. Alice begins to look through the cupboard inspecting the extra clothes inside. The other boy is quietly looking through his cupboard too but has decided to take the bed nearest the door, leaving a bed between him and the other boy. He's small and skinny, more like Alice and me and has long blond hair that curls around his ears. He's probably about my age or a little older.

"I can't believe I'm going to have to share with girls - this is awful!" The older boy moans as he lays on his bed.

"I had to share a room with my three younger sisters. The amount of crying and moaning kept me awake most nights. I'll enjoy the peace and quiet! I'm AJ, by the way, Arnold James. I gave these stuck-ups my second name, new start and all that. I never liked Arnold. What are your names?" The younger, skinny boy asks. Alice and I give our names and the other boy says his name is Damian.

"This picking an heir stuff is stupid. None of you that come from the slums are ever going to be able to fit in. I bet you can't even light a fire without magic! Why didn't they choose from the better families? Keep the riff-raff where they belong!" Damian rants spitefully.

Before any of us can retaliate, Miss Clover steps back into the room and we proceed to follow her. I look at my egg before I go, sad to leave it behind.

"Try and memorise your way please, I don't want any of you getting lost." Miss Clover says as she goes from corridor to corridor. I am not very good at directions and all the corridors look the same, the bland stone walls and overhead lighting flickering above us.

We soon get back to the main hall and see the rest of the children seated at the tables. They are all talking excitedly.

Looking around I don't see Mrs Steerly or any of the other tutors. Alice and I sit at what has become our usual place but surprisingly, AJ sits next to me. Damian goes off, talking to some other boys that look as equally well-fed as himself.

"Damian seems a bit of a character, doesn't he?" AJ asks us.

"He certainly does!" Alice agrees cheerfully.

Another group of children walk in, but the tutors are still nowhere to be seen. After a few more minutes of our little group saying very little, the servants come in with various fruits, loaves of bread and cheeses placing them on the tables. We all help ourselves hungrily.

"I wonder what happened to that boy earlier. The one Mrs Steerly hit. I don't see him in here, do you?" Alice asks quietly between mouthfuls. I try to see everyone's faces as I look around but I can't find him either.

"I don't see him, maybe they've let him go home," I say hopefully. Alice and AJ look at me with pity, we all know what fate that boy will have but none of us will say it out loud.

"I'm sure he is fine," AJ says, trying to be reassuring but his eyes shift and he fidgets in his seat nervously. "Now that we are here, do you think we are allowed to talk about... you know... magic?" He asks, looking around guiltily. I tense and stop eating. What if he asks what magic I have, what am I going to tell him? I look at Alice with my eyes wide, begging her to help.

"Maybe it's best we don't talk about it - just in case. We don't want to get into trouble and that Mrs Steerly scares me!"

Alice replies and carries on eating. I nod and stare at my plate, hoping that AJ can't see the guilt on my face.

Chapter 5

After lunch, we are all taken outside for the first time since we got here. Mr Shielding walks us through a pretty garden with budding flowers and trees in the distance. It all looks open and inviting but I still suspect that we are on the castle grounds and there will be tall walls all around us. There is little chance of escape. We are taken around the side where there is just a plain patch of grass.

"Everyone listen carefully as there is a lot to take in. This is where you will be allowed to go to exercise or socialise whilst you are here, but please don't go further than the trees, if a soldier finds you there, you will be shot - no questions asked!" Mr Shielding says. Alice and I look at each other uneasily. I realise that trying to escape will be a lot harder than I imagined. Mr Shielding continues. "As it's a nice day I thought you might appreciate being out here for your first lesson. We will start with the information regarding your eggs. You must start talking to them regularly from now on. Inside those eggs are your companions, they will help you develop your magic. It is very important that you have a strong bond with them from the start, if you don't, there is little hope of you becoming the next heir. Prince Austin's companion was a dragon and we thought they had a strong bond, but unfortunately, it wasn't enough. His dragon did not save him when he needed it. You may have noticed that the eggs were all a little different. Each egg has either green, white, red or blue marble effect to its shell. These reflect the type of creature that is in your egg. Green is an Earth creature; they typically make things grow. White is an air creature; they will be able to fly. Red is a fire creature, they typically can breathe fire and Blue is water, they can transfer their abilities to humans. They each will also have their own unique magic and abilities. This brings me on to your own magic. I am sure that despite it being forbidden for you to use your magic, some of you will have an idea of what you are capable of. From now on, you are to practice as much as possible. There will be individual assessments and tests in two weeks."

My heart rate starts to increase rapidly. That means I only have two weeks to find a way to escape or be killed when they find out I have no magic. It gives me a bit of time at least, but not enough. I feel Alice's hand slip into mine and give it a small squeeze. She knows it as much as I do; I'm doomed.

Mr Shielding goes on to explain the rules that we are to follow and the lesson schedule. We will have the same five lessons every day, Creature bonding, Magic, Etiquette, Business and History. Some we will take in our blue group that was decided by our eggs. These are also our roommates. (Oh joy, spending more time with Damian judging us all!) Others will be with another group.

"For the rest of the day, you may bond with your egg and practice your magic. Lessons will start properly tomorrow," Mr Shielding announces and then storms off back inside leaving us with many questions unanswered.

"Let's try and get back to the room and see how our eggs are," I say to Alice, who nods and follows after me. It takes many wrong turns before we finally make it back to our room and are delighted to see that it is empty.

"Are you sure you don't have any magic?" Alice asks me looking worried.

"I don't think so, how did you find out that you had it?" I ask and sit on my bed. Alice screws up her face in thought.

"Erm... I think I was quite young, about four of five. It was dark and I was scared. Then suddenly, my fingers began to feel hot and tingly and light filled the room. My mum and dad woke up and told me not to ever do it again otherwise I would be taken away from them. I still did it under the covers so they didn't see." I try and think about a time that I was scared or upset. Anything that happened that I couldn't explain or seemed strange but nothing comes to mind. Sighing loudly I lay down on the bed.

"What do you think is in here?" Alice asks curiously. Opening my eyes I see that she is sitting cross-legged by her egg, stroking it affectionately. Getting up, I sit by mine uncertainly.

"I have no idea. What are we supposed to do with it again? Just talk to it? About what?" I ask sceptically.

"About anything, I guess. Tell it about yourself, just try and sound happy," Alice replies. Facing my egg I look at it intently. The blue swirls are kind of pretty, so I trace the blue with my finger.

"So, little eggy - eggy, I've been told I have to talk to you so here it goes... My name is Amelia and I am twelve. I live...lived with my sister Caroline but now I've come to live here. I think you should come out and meet me so we can be friends," I say, trying to sound encouraging. I expect the egg to somehow respond, maybe glow like it did when I first touched it but there is nothing. Alice starts talking to hers, saying her name and age and all about her family and the jobs she did back home, rambling on and on.

"Oh!" She says suddenly and scoots closer to the egg putting both palms on the top. "I think I felt something... it was a little bump against my fingertips," she says excitedly, eyes wide with delight.

I hurriedly put both my palms on mine and wait expectantly. For a few minutes, I stay perfectly still, hardly breathing, waiting to feel something just like Alice did. Eventually, I give up. My egg is as unresponsive as the stone I thought it was. I get up and lay on my bed again. I can't help the feeling of jealousy that buzzes through my body. Alice has magic and she is already bonding with the creature in her egg. I knew that being here was a mistake and I should feel scared for my future but I didn't expect to feel so different and helpless. Tears are filling my eyes and I'm about to start crying so I get up off the bed quickly and mumble to Alice that I am going for a walk.

"Are you OK?" She shouts to me as I hurry out of the room. I don't answer as I blindly head down the corridor.

It is a long time before I finally admit to myself that I am lost. I haven't seen another child in a while and even though the corridors all look similar the walls seem to be getting even grimier the further I go. In desperation, I begin to listen at doors as I go past and even try to open a few but all are locked.

"Oh, no! What am I going to do?" I shout in frustration. All of a sudden, a door opens ahead and I'm relieved to see Miss Clover appear through the door.

"I'm so sorry Miss Clover, can you help me? I'm lost!" I beg passionately, hoping that she doesn't think that I'm up to no good and believes I genuinely need help. She looks at me suspiciously and comes closer, then looks up and down the corridor.

"Come with me Amelia, I have something to show you," she says simply and I follow her meekly and confused. After a few minutes, we go outside and down a little lane. A large barn comes into view and I get the familiar smells of the farm tingle my nose. "You should come here as often as you can, especially if you are finding certain things difficult," she says cryptically. "I will make the soldiers aware of my permission." She opens the barn door and to my surprise, there are rows of horses inside in their stables.

"Th... Thank you," I stutter out, still unsure what I am doing here.

"Talk to the horses," she says staring into my eyes for a few moments, then leaves abruptly the way we came. I stand watching her figure retreating down the lane and out of sight.

Still clueless as to why Miss Clover had brought me here, my thoughts are interrupted by a horse's whinny. Going over to the nearest stall, I'm greeted by a large black horse with a white stripe down his nose. Tentatively I stroke between his eyes. He brings its nose closer, seemingly enjoying the attention. I have never been this close to a horse before. At the farm, they were far away from the sheep and the blacksmith wouldn't let me near his.

"You are a handsome horse, aren't you?" I say to it, following Miss Clover's advice. The horse looks into my eyes deeply then nods its head up and down. "Hahaha" I laugh out loud, "You think you are too, do you? What a modest horse you are!" I say playfully. The horse nuzzles up to my shoulder as I wrap my arms around its neck. "I wish the egg was this easy to bond with," I tell it, wishing I didn't feel so helpless. A prickling feeling starts on my forehead and travels to the top and sides behind my ears. A thought pierces through my mind suddenly. 'Sing to it' I think clearly. Shaking my head in confusion, I stumble, feeling my head whoosh with dizziness. I grab hold of the stall to steady myself. After a few moments, the feeling passes. Dazed and confused I give the horse a final pat and head back down the lane and into the stone building, trying to navigate my way back. All of the other children are busily finishing their meal as I enter the meal hall.

"Where have you been?" Alice shouts reproachfully as I sit down opposite her. A servant appears, putting a plate of pasta with sauce in front of me. I don't know why, but I feel uneasy telling Alice about Miss Clover taking me to the stables. It seemed like I should keep it a secret.

"I got lost," I reply flatly, shrugging my shoulders. I pick up my cutlery and begin to eat. Alice gives me a strange look but doesn't question me further.

"What magic do you have?" AJ asks, looking at us both. I feel my stomach dip with fear and start to feel sick.

"I don't know what mine does but my fingertips glow. What about yours, AJ?" Alice asks interestedly. I take a sip of water, my mouth suddenly dry. I still get anxious talking about magic so openly.

"When I really think hard about it, I can make things lighter... sometimes they even float up in the air. It was very useful when I worked carrying bags of flour at the mill. The boss there said I was his best worker. I think he suspected I was using magic but never said anything," AJ says proudly. He then turns to me.

"How are you getting on with your egg? Alice felt something

move in hers earlier. I haven't felt anything though," I ask AJ trying to divert his attention.

"Oh wow! You felt something, Alice? That's amazing, what did it feel like?" He asks enthusiastically. I half-listen to Alice and AJ discuss their eggs whilst I finish my meal, thankful that AJ's attention is no longer on me.

After the meal, we all go up to the room and I sit on the bed whilst Alice talks to her egg some more. AJ stares at his so intently I think it must be going to burst into flames.

"Help! Help!" Someone screams from down the corridor. We all rush up and run to the room next door.

A girl is on her knees sobbing. Her egg is smashed to pieces around her on the floor, where a dead black raven lays lifelessly.

"I came back from the meal and found my egg like this. Who would do such a thing?" She wails miserably.

Alice and I step into the room, I give the girl a small pat on the shoulder sympathetically and then help her pick up the eggshell pieces. After a few minutes, Mr Shielding enters the room.

"Come with me please Laura," he asks, his gaze on the broken egg. Laura gets up sadly and follows the tutor, her sniffing can be heard all the way down the corridor.

Alice, AJ and I clean up as best we can. Alice picks up the dead raven gently and we all take it outside, not knowing what we are supposed to do with it. As Alice puts it on the grass, she makes a gasp of surprise.

"What is it?" I ask worriedly. Alice looks at the bird, a frown etching her face.

"Nothing... I just thought I felt... Never mind," she answers. We head back inside and I lead the way to where I saw Miss Clover come out of a room earlier. I knock lightly.

"Come in," a woman's voice shouts from inside. I open the door and I am relieved to see Miss Clover sitting at a desk. As we enter, I look around, the room is full of shelves of books, some piled high on every available surface.

"What can I do for you?" She says cheerily.

"Laura from the room next to ours had her egg broken. We cleaned it up as best we can and set it outside on the grass. We weren't sure what to do with it," AJ says his voice wavering with uncertainty.

"Oh, how horrible!" Miss Clover says looking deep in thought. "Thank you for letting me know, I will sort it out from here. You can all go back to your room." She stands up and ushers us out.

"Miss Clover... What will Laura do now that her raven is dead? Will she be able to get another one?" I ask timidly. Miss Clover gives a big sigh, sadness written on her face.

"I'm afraid not, you can only bond with one creature. She will have to leave," she answers resigned. We are all quiet as the realisation sinks in. Laura will become a servant or be killed, just because someone murdered her creature.

"I think we need to be careful," AJ mutters as we head back to the room. "Someone is trying to cut down the competition."

Chapter 6

As we head past the rooms, there is a lot of activity and noise. Everyone is talking about what happened to Laura's egg.

"It must have happened when we were all at dinner," a girl from her room is shouting down the corridor.

"But everyone was down there, no one was missing, were they?" A boy says next to her. AJ and Alice both look at me and frown. They know I came in late and my feeble excuse about getting lost now looks suspicious and guilty.

"I didn't, I swear!" I say as we enter our room and sit on the beds. AJ and Alice give each other nervous glances.

"Did you see anyone though? Whilst you were away?" Alice asks warily.

"No, I wasn't even near here, I was with Miss Clover. That's how I knew where her office was," I say, trying to sound believable. They both nod, considering whether what I am saying is the truth.

Damian enters the room ending the conversation. I don't trust him at all, he would be the first person to go and tell a tutor that he thought it was me. Now that Laura has had hers smashed and her creature cruelly taken away from her, I feel a sudden protectiveness against mine. It isn't just the threat of if it was harmed. I feel like it would hurt me inside if anything happened to it. I sit infront of it and tenderly stroke its shell, wishing once again that I could feel it move.

"Why are you lot so miserable?" Damian asks us, seeing the sad looks on our faces. "You can't be upset about a girls egg getting smashed, this is good news. One less out of the competition. You peasants should be grateful; you're never going to make it to the end without a miracle," he states smugly.

"How can you be so mean?" I shout angrily, storming towards him with my fists clenched. "Laura could be dead by now, but all you care about is this competition!"

"Calm down, you idiot!" Damian responds, glaring at me with hatred.

Alice grabs me roughly by the arm and pulls me to the back of the room, as far away from Damian as we can get. I take a deep breath, trying to calm down but I am shaking with fury.

For the rest of the evening, we all sit and whisper to our eggs until it is time to go to bed. Damian doesn't look at me at all and I happily stay out of his way.

The next morning, nervousness can be felt all around as we enter the meal hall. This is our first official day of learning. When we have all finished our breakfast of porridge, all four tutors and Mrs Steerly enter the hall.

"Everyone get your eggs and come back down here," Mrs Steerly instructs in her usual chilling voice that sends shivers down my spine.

We all rush out and down the corridors to our rooms and slowly pick up our eggs. We then get back to the meal hall as fast as we can without dropping them.

When Damian, Alice, AJ and I are all back we stand in front of Miss Clover. Hopefully, she will be taking the class and not the awful Mrs Steerly. My wishes are heard as Miss Clover directs us to a room only a few doors away.

We enter the small, cramped room with just one large table in the centre with eight chairs surrounding it. We all take a seat and place our eggs on the table. Fortunately, Alice sits between me and Damian. Miss Clover sits at the head of the table.

"This lesson is 'Creature bonding'. It will become more interesting when your eggs eventually hatch but for now, you are to continue to talk to them at every opportunity," she says.

"Miss Clover, what creature will be in our eggs?" Alice asks curiously. We have all discussed this back in our room, but none of us came out with any ideas.

"Well, there are four main creatures it could be. A toad, a water nymph, a merturtle or a sea serpent. You will have to bond with it to see what magic each of them has but some can go invisible or heal for example," she answers.

"What are nymph's and merturtle's?" AJ asks, flushing with embarrassment. Damian gives out a small snort which he smothers before Miss Clover glares at him.

"Nymphs are small creatures, similar to a fairy but they don't have wings. They don't have to live in water but they are attracted to it. Merturtle's are mermaids with a turtle shell back, they can breathe out of the water but find it difficult to get around. Both nymphs and merturtle's like to sing and their magic is stronger when they do. A sea serpent is a water snake. Its hiss is the same as the others singing just not quite so pleasant. It sleeps in water but spends most of the day out of it," she answers. We all look at each other with our mouths open, trying to guess which creature is in our egg. "The rest of this time you should spend trying to bond with your egg, I'll be back soon," she states and heads out the door.

"Bet mine is the snake!" Damian announces eagerly looking at his egg with glee.

"I don't care as long as it's not a toad," Alice says with a shudder.

Taking my egg I think about what to say, but my mind goes blank. I feel silly and embarrassed talking to it in front of Damian. I whisper to my egg softly. I don't say anything exciting, just what we had for breakfast and asking it what creature it might be, hoping that it will respond.

We sit and whisper to our eggs for what seems like a long time, but we quickly get bored and run out of things to say so we are mostly silent, not daring to say anything too loudly in case Miss Clover is standing outside the door listening.

Eventually, Miss Clover comes back into the room and we all shift guiltily. She looks at us individually and frowns, then sits back down.

"This next class is Magic. Now I understand that you won't have had much practice and have limited ability at best but it's important to practice as much as possible. It is also important that you listen to what your body is trying to tell you. When your magic presents itself, it is usually the sensations in your body that come out first and then the magic manifests itself. So, I want you to all close your eyes for a few minutes. Take a deep breath in and slowly release it. Focus your mind on your toes... then your ankles... your calves... your knees... and work all the way up your body. Focusing on every muscle and joint. Try and release all the tension you are experiencing," she instructs, breathing deeply along with us.

I try and do what Miss Clover is saying, but just being here is making me tense. I need to get out somehow, it's not going to take her long to realise that I have no magic, nothing is manifesting, there is no ability. Sneakily, I try to open one eye to look at the others around me. Miss Clover has got up and is walking around with her back to us, still talking about every body part. Alice looks completely chilled next to me. Looking at AJ makes me jerk back suddenly; he is holding onto his chair and hovering! Miss Clover notices my sudden movement and rests her eyes on AJ.

"Oh, well done!" She congratulates loudly, clapping her hands together.

AJ opens his eyes and both him and the chair he is holding bump back down to the floor. AJ looks happy and excited.

Alice looks slightly thoughtful but Damian looks thunderous, his eyes squinting at AJ with loathing.

"Now, all of you go and take a walk or find somewhere quiet and repeat the exercise I just told you. It's better to be on your own without any distractions. I'll take your eggs back upstairs for you and I'll meet you in the meal hall in an hour," she instructs. She then holds her palms out in front of her facing upward. Our eggs jerk up swiftly to head height and Miss Clover walks out of the room, the eggs floating after her.

Wow," I say impressed by the tutor's magic. "She made that look easy." Damian barges past us and through the door.

"That's because it is easy!" He says and races down the corridor.

"I wonder what magic Damian has?" AJ asks curiously. "Maybe it's just the ability to be as mean as he can possibly be!"

Alice, AJ and I laugh together as we head outside. We each go in different directions trying to find a quiet spot. I consider sitting down and doing what was asked of me, but this seems a good opportunity to look around. I am on my own and there isn't anyone else in sight. There might be a way to escape if only I can find it. Hastily looking around, I go as close to the trees as I dare and begin to walk alongside the tree line. I squint, trying to look amongst the trees but all I see is darkness, I can't even see if there is a wall close by. Up ahead is the garden so I walk towards that trying to retrace the steps of our first day here. We must have come in through a gate before going to the hall,

I just need to find it. I am about to make my way back near the hall when a movement startles me from behind a tree. Putting my hand up to block the sun from my eyes, I look towards it, my heart pounding.

"Tom?" I yell looking straight at him. Tom comes out from behind the tree, he has an egg in his hand with swirls of red. Seeing me he smiles brightly.

"Amelia, what are you doing here?" He asks happily. I look at him thoughtfully. I wonder if I can trust him? Maybe he could help me? Hurrying up to him I make a quick decision.

"I'm trying to find a way to escape," I whisper, looking around me frantically just in case we are overheard. Tom knows me, he is from my village, surely he will understand my need for freedom. Tom's face quickly changes to one of concern.

"Do you know what they will do if they catch you?" He asks, panic clear in his voice.

"I don't... I don't have any magic; I don't have any choice," I whisper shaking my head rapidly. Tom looks at me, his still swollen eye as wide as it can go giving me a glimpse of blue. He doesn't say anything for a long time, shifting the egg from hand to hand. Panic starts to engulf my body, did I do right in telling him or have I made a big mistake?

"There might be a way..." He starts to say, but he cuts off and looks behind me.

Turning around I see Mr Majors, the tutor for the red group coming out of one of the doors. I turn back to look at Tom but he has gone! Looking around desperately, I try to find which direction he went but I can't see him - he's vanished! What was he going to tell me? Did he know a way out? But if he did then why is he still here? Mr Majors sees me and heads in my direction. I try not to look guilty as he comes towards me.

"What are you doing out here?" He demands.

"Miss Clover said I could come out and find a quiet place to practise my magic," I reply as confidently as I can muster.

"It's time you went back inside. I hope you have been using your time wisely Amelia, everyone else is working hard to better themselves. I hope you are too," he says with an evil glint to his eye. I don't think he wants me to do well at all but I don't dare challenge him, I just want to get away from him as quickly as I can.

"Yes, of course, Mr Majors. I had better get inside then, I don't want to be late," I say innocently. I walk as quickly as I can, but I have an uneasy feeling he is watching my every move as I go back inside.

Miss Clover collects us from the hall and takes us to our next lesson. When we get there, I'm surprised to see that we will be sharing this class with the white group. I only recognise one girl who I think is named Mia. I saw her yesterday talking about Laura's smashed egg. We all sit around the table with Miss Clover and Mr Shielding standing at the front.

"This lesson is Etiquette, obviously if you become the next heir your life will change dramatically. There will be a lot of events that will take place and you must not let the Royal Family down," Mr Shielding informs us.

He goes on and on about manners, kindness, what not to say...I look at Alice several times throughout his speech but she is eagerly looking at the tutor engrossed in what he is saying. Looking around the room I get a pang of sadness as I remember that Laura should be in this group with us. I try and concentrate but I already know this. My mum and dad instilled manners into us from when we were young. Just as I feel my mind go numb with boredom the lesson is over and we go to lunch.

Chapter 7

The rest of the day is uneventful, we learn about Business and History - both lessons are with the white group. By this point I really don't want to become a royal, it seems mind-numbingly dull but the alternative is much worse, so I try and take it seriously. My mind often drifts to my conversation with Tom wondering what he was going to say. It's at the evening meal that something unexpected happens.

"WHERE IS IT?" An older boy with spiky red hair and freckles comes storming into the hall screaming at the room. Everyone stops eating and looks at him, confusion on all our faces. "Someone has taken my egg, give it back now or there will be trouble!" He shouts looking around the room. Everyone looks around, expecting the guilty person to own up. When no one says anything, he marches out of the room and down the hall.

"Do you think someone's taken it and smashed it, just like Laura's?" Alice says quietly to AJ and me.

"It looks like it," AJ replies looking uncomfortable.

An image comes into my head of when I saw Tom earlier carrying an egg outside. The egg had red swirls. I look around and see Tom on the other table, he definitely isn't in the white group otherwise I would've just seen him in class, so that makes him in red or green. Thinking back to when they were announcing the groups, I remember that Tom hadn't been called before Alice and I. Mr Majors had taken red group, Mr Shielding the white. With a gasp, I realise that Tom must be in green. Tom had a red egg! Tom must have taken it! He must have smashed Laura's too - and I have just told him that I have no magic! With a flood of terror, I realise that I shouldn't have told him my secret. Tom can't be trusted. After hearing my gasp and seeing the look on my face Alice and AJ know that something is wrong. I quickly shake my head.

"Not here," I mutter and try to eat the rest of my food.

Annoyingly, when we get back to our room Damian is already there talking to his egg, looking at it worriedly.

"We don't dare leave them now, do we? Not until they are hatched and can defend themselves," he says looking vulnerable, all smugness gone from his face. He is right. How can we leave our eggs unprotected when someone, probably Tom, is going around taking or smashing them?

Sitting down by my egg, I will it to hatch. Desperation has overridden any embarrassment I have about talking to it in front of Damian. Somehow, for this fleeting moment, I feel like we are all in this together, battling against the enemy. After a while and nothing happening, I give a big sigh.

"Anyone having any luck?" I ask everyone. AJ and Damian shake their heads miserably.

"Actually, I think I'm getting somewhere, I've felt it move several times now," Alice says proudly.

"What are you saying to make it move?" AJ asks, the look of frustration clear on his face.

"Nothing really, just talking," Alice replies. All the rest of us look at her disappointed. We don't know what we are doing and it shows. "I wonder what is in there, if it's a nymph or a merturtle, what do you think their singing sounds like?" She asks us.

Just then I think back to when I was with the horse and I went dizzy. I thought that I heard a voice tell me to sing to the egg. I hadn't thought of it since.

"If they like singing themselves, do you think that they might like it if we sing?" I ask apprehensively.

I look at the others, AJ looks at his egg intently and starts to sing. It is a lullaby that is quite popular in our village, mostly sung to babies to get them to sleep. It talks of a new day, being free to run and play. We all join in, our voices mingling together in harmony. It doesn't take long for my palms to start to feel the stirring of something moving inside.

"I can feel it!" I shout excitedly. I can't believe that it has worked! How did I hear this advice? The thoughts are cleared from my head as I feel the movement again. I can't believe how happy I am. I suddenly feel very connected to my egg. AJ and Damian are still singing determinedly, their voices becoming strained with the effort.

"Eurgh! This is stupid, Amelia, you are stupid!" Damian yells as he gets up and storms out of the room. Our brief closeness coming to an end.

Chapter 8

We wake up to screaming. The piercing sound echo's loudly down the corridor.

"What's happened now?" I ask, fearing the answer as I cover my ears. We all run down the hall trying to locate the sound, passing all the doors until we get to red group's room. All the other children are huddled around the doorway trying to see what the commotion is. Being small and slight has always been an advantage for me, so I slip under people's arms and squeeze through small gaps pushing them out of the way. One of the girls, probably the same age as me with long blonde hair, is staring at her egg. At first, I don't understand why she is screaming. The egg is still there and looks fine. It is only after a few moments that I realise what's happening, there is a crack at the top and a piece of shell is moving.

"It's hatching!" A boy shouts excitedly.

We all watch as something slowly emerges, bits of shell falling to the floor. The blonde girl picks bits from the egg until we all see the head of a beautiful red and gold bird.

"It's a phoenix!" She shouts, her voice full of wonder.

I'm sure I'm not the only one that feels a surge of jealousy as she pets her phoenix's head and it nuzzles up to her. Suddenly,

I remember my own egg and terror washes over me. I have left it in our room unprotected! Squeezing back through all the children, I run as fast as I can back to my egg. I give a sigh of relief as I see they are all still intact.

We all take our eggs down to breakfast with us, not daring to leave them unattended. I decide to keep it with me all the time, carrying it in its nest to keep it warm.

Creature bonding is a bit more fun, knowing that one egg has already hatched gives us a boost to try our hardest. Our little group talk and sing to our eggs joyfully. AJ can now feel some movement in his, but Damian sits and sulks moodily as his egg doesn't respond.

During our magic lesson, Miss Clover sets the same tasks as before, so each of us go in different directions. As I know I don't have magic, this is a waste of time for me, so I go and explore the grounds again. Miss Clover watches over our eggs whilst we are out.

I keep a sharp lookout for Tom, half dreading seeing him but needing to know what he was trying to tell me yesterday. I'm surprised that the soldiers haven't come for me yet, if he is the one stealing and smashing eggs to reduce the competition then I'm easy prey. All he has to do is tell a tutor my secret and I'd be a servant in minutes, maybe even killed. I've managed to hide that I have no magical ability for a few days, they would probably kill me for that, just because I wasn't honest and it makes them look bad that they haven't noticed yet. I hope if they ever do find out, Miss Clover isn't punished as she is the only tutor here I trust. She took me to the horse and that made me think about singing to the egg.

Thinking about the horse now I decide to go over to the stables. I didn't properly look around the area so there might be something I missed.

Before I open the barn door, I look around eagerly trying to find a wall I could climb over or a gate to the outside. All I see is a large field with the castle in the distance, the forest surrounding us all. Surely the forest doesn't wrap around the whole of the castle? There must be a wall somewhere?

Entering the barn, I am greeted by the familiar black horse with its white nose. He eagerly stretches his head and neck towards me, trying to get a close as possible.

"Good morning horsey," I say to him affectionately as I roughly rub his nose. Near the stall, I notice a bag hanging on a peg. Looking inside, I find It's filled with sugar lumps. The horse snorts loudly and tosses his head up and down excitedly. "Is this what you want handsome horsey?" I ask him in a silly sweet voice I only use for animals. I take a few lumps of sugar from the bag putting one on the flat of my palm, making it easy for the horse to eat. He gobbles it up quickly.

The horses in the other stalls start neighing and stamping, hoping they will get a treat.

I go over to the bag and I am just about to get more to feed them when my vision starts to blur, dark circling the edges.

My head begins to prickle and hurt.

"Please, Please, Please," I hear, the voices surrounding me scream. I fall to the floor too dizzy to stand, the straw prickling my hands. I take a few deep breaths trying to calm down for my vision to return to normal. I don't know what just happened, but I need to get outside to the fresh air. Leaving the sugar lumps on the floor I stumble through the door. The suns warmth hits my face and the breeze seems to wipe clean the dizziness I felt. I look towards the barn once again. Why is it that when I go inside, I become unwell? Am I allergic to horses? I feel fine now I am outside.

Slowly opening the barn door again I look inside hesitantly. The horses are all quietly standing in their stalls. I pick up the sugar lumps, expecting to hear the voices once again but everything is fine, there is no sound or dizziness. I take a sugar lump and head over to the familiar black and white horse. I give it another lump of sugar and pat his nose. I stay stroking the horse for another few minutes but thankfully, the tingling in my head and the dizziness doesn't return. Confused I head back to the building.

Over the next few days more and more children's eggs start to hatch but none in the blue group seem to be in any hurry. During meals, the sight of Gnomes, Fairies, Phoenix, Ravens and Pixies becomes a regular sight. One boy even has a Gargoyle that turns to stone periodically. Lessons for us stay the same, except I look on jealously as Alice's and AJ's magic powers get stronger. We still don't know what Damian's are yet, but with every day he gets surlier and more loathsome. I try to hide my growing hate for him but we argue constantly if we are in the same room for longer than a few minutes. His superior nature winds me up and grates on my nerves.

"Just ignore him," AJ says to me one morning as we head down to breakfast. "He only says it to wind you up and it works every time. He just loves making trouble," he says soothingly. AJ and I have become quite close since we have been here. Alice has become obsessed with her egg and her lessons. I can understand she wants to be the best as she can be - her life depends on it. I just miss the closeness we had. The more magic she has the more there seems to be a greater distance between us.

As we walk into the meal hall we are greeted by an abundance of children and creatures, It seems that almost all of the eggs have hatched overnight. I clutch onto mine and look at it. There isn't even a little crack, the blue swirls and rough edges are still just the same as when I first picked it up. We walk into the dining hall and I am just about to take a seat when my head begins to tingle and ache and my sight blurs. I quickly put the egg on the table before blackness engulfs my vision.

All I can hear is a loud humming noise as though a thousand people are all talking at once. I press my hands over my ears tightly trying to muffle the sound but the dizziness keeps growing so much that I collapse onto the floor.

The last thing I feel is a sudden weight on my chest before the darkness takes over.

Chapter 9

The first thing I notice when I awake is the smell; it's strong and unpleasant. Nothing like I've encountered before. Blinking my eyes open I realise that I'm in an empty room with a few other beds. They all have stark white pillows and covers. I look around curiously. On the bedside table lays my egg but it looks strange. Panic overwhelms me as I shoot out of bed. The egg is broken and there's nothing inside! Heartbroken, I slump back down miserably. This is it then. I must have broken my egg as I fell, I'll become a servant or killed. Putting my face in my hands, I sob. I knew my fate would end like this and yet I always hoped that by some miracle I would be able to prevent it, that even without magic I would be able to escape.

When I hear the creaking of the door opening I don't look up, I don't want to see the soldiers that I know have come for me. I don't want to be roughly grabbed and taken away. Sadly, I realise that I will probably never see Alice or AJ again unless one of them becomes the next heir and I become a servant. I might be able to see glances of them in their new life with their magical abilities strong, fascinating and majestic.

"Come along dear, none of that. There's nothing wrong with you now," a kind, motherly voice says from across the room.

Looking up, I see a round, elderly woman. Her grey hair is tightly curled under a white cap. She is also wearing a white apron but bizarrely of all, there is a bright blue snake wrapped tightly around her wrist like some sort of bracelet!

"This belongs to you," she says and holds out her snake covered wrist. The snake unwinds itself and slithers onto the end of my bed.

"Aaah!" I shriek, hitting the headboard as I back away from it. As I look into its eyes I feel a pull from deep inside me. I can't explain the feeling that fizzes throughout my body, it feels like I haven't been using my body properly for all my life, that now, I am complete. I feel stronger than I did before, like I could take on anything just as long as this snake is next to me.

Tentatively, I hold out my arm and the snake wraps itself around my wrist. As it touches me for the first time, there is a spark of recognition; of a connection. This is my creature that I have been talking to and loving and nurturing from the egg.

"At last, we meet," I hear, but the voice wasn't spoken out loud. The hissing voice was spoken in my head. Binking rapidly I try to understand what is going on.

"You've got a good one there," the kindly woman says. "As soon as you fainted it cracked out the egg with super speed and wrapped itself around you hissing at anyone that came near. Took us a good hour to convince it that we were there to help you."

Looking at the snake again, its beady black eyes don't look

menacing or scary. They have a calming quality to them, making me feel safe and protected.

"What are you going to call him?" The woman asks beaming.

I have never named anything before. Caroline and I have never had any pets and the sheep I worked with just had numbers. I try to think of something but my mind goes blank.

"My name is Azure," the hidden voice hisses in my head.

"Azure," I say out loud to the woman.

"Perfect!" She beams and heads out the door. "You may go now; you are perfectly fine."

Still wearing the same clothes as when I fell, I follow the woman and head down the corridor, my wrist heavy with the weight of the snake wrapped around it. I find my way quickly to the meal hall but there is no one around. I have no idea what time it is so guess that the others are probably in lessons as it is still light outside. Firstly, I head towards the room we have lessons with Miss Clover but she is nowhere to be seen so think that they must be with the white group having afternoon lessons. I must have missed lunch. I stand outside the door not knowing what to do. Do I knock and then enter? Or just walk in? I feel embarrassed as I try to decide what to do.

"Knock, wait for a command and then walk in and apologise for being late," the hissing voice in my head says which I now realise must be Azure.

"How are you talking to me?" I ask him.

"You can talk to animals... didn't you know?" Azure says

matter-of-factly.

I think back to the horses. How I got a prickly feeling in my head and the dizziness as I heard the voices. Then how there seemed to be too many voices in my head when I went into the meal hall. There were a lot of animals. All the creatures of the children. They were all talking and I could hear them. I do feel a slight prickling when Azure talks to me but I am not dizzy. I am about to ask him more questions but the door opens suddenly and children push past me as they come out of the room. Stepping back, I let them pass.

"Amelia! There you are, we were so worried!" Alice squeals and reaches out to hug me with the arm not clutching her egg. She stops suddenly and looks at my wrist with Azure wrapped around it. "Will that thing let me near you now? It nearly bit me earlier when I saw you on the floor." AJ comes up behind Alice and smiles at me warmly.

"Glad to see you back on your feet," he says cheekily.

"Yes, he's fine," I say to Alice and roll my eyes at AJ. "What did I miss?" I ask.

"You missed all your lessons; it's evening meal now. We learned about place setting in Etiquette so you will need to catch up on that and Business was something about trading with other islands. History was more boring royals that lived hundreds of years ago." Alice recounts.

"Alice! You are missing the most vital news... One of the red groups had their phoenix stolen!" AJ shouts looking at Alice reproachfully.

"Stolen?" I ask him confused, bringing Azure closer to my body protectively, wrapping my other hand around him.

"Yeah, a boy named Robert. Left his phoenix in his room this morning and went back to lunch and it was gone. No one can find it. Between you fainting and the missing phoenix, it's been a very interesting day! The tutors keep questioning him. Asking something about if he can still feel it... It's all very odd. He's still here having lessons; they haven't taken him away yet."

I try and process everything that's happened as we walk into the meal hall. As we enter, the harsh racket of what sounds like a hundred voices talking all at once stops me dead in my tracks. I slap my hands over my ears to try and deaden the noise. I start to feel the prickling in my head and back away down the corridor.

"I can't go in, I can't go in," I say frantically shaking my head.

"What's wrong?" Alice says worriedly, rushing over. I'm trying to breathe deeply, to stop myself from fainting again so don't answer her. I feel Azure slither up my arm wrapping himself around my head as though I am wearing him like a crown. The movement distracts me from my distress.

"You must try and concentrate on your friends and not everything around you. Try and focus just on them, I will help you until you learn to block them," Azure hisses to me. I look at Alice's face. Her eyes are wide with concern. AJ is staring at

Azure uneasily, probably worried he's going to get attacked. I take a few deep breaths.

"I'll be OK," I say trying to sound reassuring as I attempt to walk back into the meal hall, trying my hardest to focus on getting to the table and sitting down. My legs are wobbly but I get there. Alice sits next to me, with AJ opposite. I try and focus on AJ's features. His curly blond hair and his deep blue eyes, a shade lighter than Azure.

Somehow, I get through the meal, there are a few hazy moments but I try and focus on the conversation which is mostly about the missing phoenix. Afterwards, we head upstairs to the bedroom where Alice and AJ both put their eggs back on their nests gently. Azure slithers off me, across the floor and with a tiny 'plop' gets into the tank of water by the window. He then curls up under a rock and appears to fall asleep. My wrist feels lighter without him curled around it; I miss his comforting weight.

"What's it like having your creature?" Alice asks a touch of jealousy in her voice. I realise I haven't told her my news.

"It's great... there's a real connection but more than that, I can hear him talk!" I say excitedly, my words coming out in a rush. "That's why I fainted earlier. I can hear them all talk so it's just so overwhelming! I have magic! I can talk to animals!" Alice's mouth hangs open as she listens to my speech.

"You didn't know you had magic?" AJ asks confused.

"No, I thought that they'd made a mistake," I tell him. All I've thought about since I got here was trying to escape as I didn't think I had magic. Now that I do, should I stay? I sit down on my bed and think about my options. I could stay and be in the running to be the heir, or more likely become a servant or be killed. Azure would be taken from me if I fail. I couldn't bear for that to happen. A feeling of dread consumes me. Even if I do become the next heir, I may not have the power to stop my friends becoming servants or being killed. Their creatures will be taken from them. I panic as I think about it - I just can't do that! "We all have to escape and the sooner the better," I tell them both.

Damian walks quietly into the room, interrupting our conversation. Alice and AJ start talking to their eggs in their usual desperate manner hoping that he didn't overhear our conversation. We all stop as we notice that Damian isn't carrying his egg, we watch with interest as he goes over to the tank and drops something into it. Damian has a merturtle! It looks like a very small boy with long green hair and blue skin but has a dark green shell on its back and a tail. It swims around happily in the tank, its scales glistening. Azure opens his eyes briefly, looks at the merturtle then settles back down.

"Why have I got this stupid merturtle and you have a snake? Did you swap our eggs when I was asleep?" Damian asks accusingly as he sits on the bed in a huff.

"Don't be daft Damian, you wouldn't feel a bond if it wasn't yours. That's why you can only have one. Amelia's snake attacked anyone that went near her this morning, that's a true bond," Alice says knowledgeably.

"What was all that about anyway? Fancied the day off? The stress of working too tiring for you? Maybe you had better quit now," Damian says nastily. I try to ignore him as AJ keeps telling me but I can feel the frustration and anger build inside me. Azure swims to the top of the tank and slithers towards me, to my surprise he rises up ready to strike by my side.

"Wow, calm down you loony!" Damian says sounding scared and backing away with his arms up in surrender. "No need to start a fight over it."

Alice is beaming in delight as she looks between Azure and Damian, whilst AJ looks completely shocked. I look at Azure appreciatively. No one is going to be able to mess with me while he's around.

"Ah, Ah, Aah!" Alice starts screaming breaking the tension in the room. I rush over and see what the matter is, Azure, following swiftly. "My egg! It's beginning to hatch!" We all watch as a faint crack appears at the top of the egg, some of the shell beginning to move. More cracks start to appear and bits of shell fall onto the bed. Gently, Alice removes some of the bigger pieces and a blue head pops out of the top. It has a very wide shaped head, with long, stringy hair. It uses its big hands and feet to climb out and walks over to Alice. It then raises its arms, just like a toddler would for its mother. Alice looks at it with pure affection and lifts it onto her lap. "It's a water nymph!" She says proudly. We all watch as she immediately bonds with the nymph with tears of joy glistening in her eyes. Damian storms out of the room muttering to himself.

"COME ON HATCH!" AJ shouts to his egg giving it a little shake and staring at it with disgust. "Why is mine the last one?" He asks frustratedly putting it down on its nest. Alice is still mesmerised with her nymph and doesn't even look as though she heard him.

"I think there are still a few others that haven't hatched," I say feebly and sit on the bed, Azure curling up beside me. I get a familiar prickle in my head.

"It's ready to hatch now, Amelia. Go and tell it to come out, it will listen to you," I frown at Azure, not understanding.

"What do you mean?" I ask him out loud in confusion.

"I didn't say anything," AJ says, looking at me strangely.

"Oh no, sorry, I was talking to Azure. He said that I should tell the creature in your egg to hatch - that it's ready." AJ looks at me as though I have gone mad and then looks at his egg.

"Give it a go, if you like," he says, shrugging.

I slowly go over to AJ's egg. I think about stoking it but I feel that would be inappropriate somehow. None of us touch each other's eggs.

"Hey... If you are ready to hatch, then AJ would like to see you. Could you come out...please," I ask it hesitantly.

I look at it but nothing happens. I'm about to turn around and tell Azure off for making me look silly when I start to hear a small sound. AJ grabs hold of the egg and puts it on his bed softly. Alice, still holding her nymph comes over and we all watch as the creature emerges. It is another merturtle, but this one has bright yellow hair. It gives me a big scowl when it sees me.

"I was just having a nap!" I hear it say accusingly and then it looks at AJ adoringly.

We don't say much to each other the rest of the evening, everyone is too busy bonding with their creatures. It's weird as I can hear what the other creatures are saying but AJ and Alice can't. It's like hearing a private conversation. Alice's nymph is very talkative and there's a very strong bond between them.

Alice, settles into bed with her nymph, called Dora, snuggled up to her, the rest of the creatures prefer to be in the water to sleep. Looking at Alice I feel a little jealous. Bedtime is always the hardest time for me as it makes me think of Caroline. I wonder what she would think if she were here. If you take away the constant threat of becoming a servant or being killed, I must admit that I am enjoying being here with my friends and now our creatures.

Chapter 10

'Creature bonding' lesson is a lot different now that all our creatures have hatched. Damian still looks disappointedly at his merturtle but the rest of us are very happy. No one could be more elated than Alice. She never lets Dora out of her sight. AJ has decided to call his merturtle 'Rio' and Damian has called his 'Melvin'.

"This is an exciting day!" Miss Clover says looking around us proudly. "Now all of the creatures are hatched, this is where the fun and hard work really starts. You must continue to bond with your creature at every opportunity but now you must also find out what abilities your creature has. As they are water creatures, they will also be able to share their magic with you. So, if they can turn invisible, for example, you will be able to turn invisible too when they touch you. It won't be easy to find out their magic as they need to develop it - just like you had to do." We all look excitedly at our creatures wondering what their abilities are. It occurs to me that I could just ask Azure and the others.

"I don't know what they are, we have to develop them together," Azure responds, reading my thoughts. "You don't have to talk to me out loud, you can just think what you need to say and I can hear you."

"Do you hear everything that is in my head?" I ask him, feeling a bit embarrassed.

"No," he replies. "Only what you let me hear. At the moment, I only hear if you want to ask me a question or if your emotions are heightened. You probably are doing it without meaning to but don't worry, we will develop this more," he says reassuringly. Relieved, I continue to listen to Miss Clover.

"I will now be teaching you individually starting from tomorrow. The rest of the time you will work independently. Damian, you will be with me first, AJ will be next, then Alice and then Amelia. Please stick close so I don't have to waste time trying to find you. There are a few empty rooms next to this one that you can use. At first, try and show your magic to your creature and it will pick up what you are trying to achieve. For the rest of this class and the next Magic lesson, you may work independently," she instructs and then leaves the room smiling brightly.

"I thought they said they were going to train us here? Miss Clover is awful, she just tells us to go and work on our own most of the time. I bet the others are going to have developed their magic much more than we have," Damian complains loudly, grabbing his merturtle and angrily rushing out of the door.

"He has got a point," AJ agrees regretfully, following Damian.

"Do you think all the tutors are teaching the same?" Alice

asks me timidly slowly getting up. We head out the door as I think about what to say. I like Miss Clover and I definitely wouldn't want Mr Majors or Mrs Steerly instead of her but I don't think we have advanced as much as I expected since being here.

"Maybe," I answer feeling guilty.

Alice says she's going to the garden with Dora so I decide to head over to the stables, now that I understand my magic it would be nice to go and talk to the horses properly.

"I hear something," Azure says to me tightly wrapped around my wrist.

"What?" I ask cautiously. I then start to hear it too. It is a voice that sounds far away. Walking slowly, I listen carefully.

"Help!" I hear further down the corridor. I start to jog, pausing at every door, eventually reaching one that I think the voice is coming from. Pulling the handle, I find that it's locked, so I pull it again as hard as I can but it doesn't budge. Frustrated, I keep trying. Then to my amazement, Azure makes a loud hissing sound and glows a bright blue. I don't understand what's happening but the door bursts open.

"Let me go first," Azure says protectively, slithering inside. I follow closely behind. It is dark in this room as there are no windows. I have to wait for my eyes to adjust before I see it. There is a phoenix tied with a chain to the floor, its feathers looking ruffled and scruffy.

"What are you doing in here?" A commanding voice behind

us demands. It is Mrs Steerly. A shiver runs down my spine as I look at her. She sees the phoenix behind me and frowns.

"Soldiers! I need soldiers here right now!" She shouts, her voice echoing around. Azure gets in front of me and rises up, ready to attack.

Three burly soldiers appear in the room as if from nowhere. Panicking I look at Mrs Steerly, her face is grim and determined. Why has she called the soldiers? I haven't done anything! Azure tries to bite them as they come towards me but they have shields and batons. The snake strikes out bravely but one of the soldiers hits him hard with his baton and flings him to one side, where his beautiful blue body lies unmoving on the ground.

"Azure! Are you OK?" I cry, begging him to respond but I don't hear anything at all. One soldier picks up Azure's limp body, whilst another grabs me roughly and pushes me infront of him. We arrive at a room nearby which seems to be Mrs Steerly's office. Roughly, I'm thrown into a chair and I wince as my back hits the hard wood. Mrs Steerly sits rigidly behind her desk glaring at me. Tears roll down my cheek as I look around and see Azure still dangling from the soldier's hand behind me.

"So, you are the thief? Breaking and stealing eggs. Capturing a phoenix. Mr Majors told me that you've been sneaking around and we should keep an eye on you. What do you have to say before I put you to death?" She asks with a smug look on her face.

"I haven't done anything! I heard a noise coming from the room, when I looked inside, I found the phoenix!" I cry desperately, trying to make her believe me, my heart thudding hard in my chest.

"I DON'T BELIEVE YOU!" She shouts at me venomously.

"I heard him, I heard the phoenix cry out for help, please believe me. I didn't take anything!" I wail, tears spilling from my eyes. I wipe them away as I look at her pleadingly. She suddenly looks a little unsure, narrowing her eyes at me.

"You heard the phoenix cry out? You can hear animals speaking?" She asks me through gritted teeth. I am almost afraid to admit it. Owning up to having magic has always been dangerous, but I sense having this ability won't please her. However, it is the only way that I can clear my name.

"Yes," I whisper looking down afraid to meet her cold, hard eyes. She gets up so suddenly that I flinch, thinking she's about to hit me but to my relief, she passes my chair and opens her door.

"Get me Mr Shielding!" She orders and I see a soldier hurrying off. Slamming the door, she comes back sitting menacingly on the edge of the table, glaring at me. "You think that you have this extraordinary magical power to talk to animals, do you? This rare gift that is only found in noble blood? We will find out and when we do, I will enjoy killing that little serpent of yours, making you feel the agony of a broken bond and then, eventually, I will kill you too," she says with glee. The tension grows in the silence as we wait for Mr Shielding's knock on the door.

"Come in," Mrs Steerly says almost sweetly. She looks maliciously at me as she welcomes the tutor, delighted at what my fate could entail. "Mr Shielding, apparently Amelia here, this nobody from the slums thinks that she can talk to animals. Can you confirm that she is lying so that I can punish her swiftly for stealing please?"

Mr Shielding gives me a thoughtful look before reaching into his jacket, I lean back in my chair expecting some sort of weapon but I am surprised when he pulls out a small, very ruffled looking raven.

Just then the door bursts open and Miss Clover and Alice hurry into the room and stand in front of me protectively. Miss Clover looks hard at each of the tutor's, her eyes resting on Azure.

"Alice, can you please see to Amelia's creature whilst I talk to the others," she asks tensely and looks at Mrs Steerly, her stare blazing with fury.

"What are you doing here Miss Clover, this doesn't concern you," Mrs Steerly accuses harshly.

"I am Amelia's tutor; it definitely does concern me!" She practically spits out.

Alice rushes over to Azure and gently takes him from the soldier's grasp and lays him on the floor. Kneeling down, she closes her eyes. Her fingers glow bright blue, just like they did when she first showed me her magic. She gently touches Azure, and he moves slightly.

Panicking, I race over and sit beside him. Slowly his tail begins to curl and he wraps himself into a ball looking at me with his beady eyes.

"I'm OK, can you thank Alice for me?" Azure says weakly. I look at Alice with confusion.

"Azure thanks you. What did you do?" I ask quietly.

"I can heal," she answers, looking pleased. She stands up and scoops Azure gently into her arms. "I will take him to the tank if that's OK?" She asks Miss Clover, not looking at the rest of the tutors. Miss Clover nods briskly and Alice leaves the room giving me a small comforting smile. I know she will look after my snake but him being away from me makes me uneasy.

"Let's get on with it, shall we?" Mrs Steerly asks happily. Walking over to the chair, I sit back down apprehensively. Mr Shielding stands in front of me with a kind expression.

"Amelia, all you have to do is tell me what this raven is saying then we will all know if you're telling the truth," he says calmly, clutching the bird tightly.

The raven is looking around the room, jerkily moving its head from side to side. Not hearing anything, I look at Miss Clover for help and she nods encouragingly. Out of the corner of my eye I can see that Mrs Steerly's smile has got wider. I try and concentrate on the bird but it is silent.

"Well?" Mrs Steerly shouts exasperated. I look down as tears fill my eyes.

"I'm sorry, it didn't say anything but please believe me. I am telling the truth!" I cry out.

"That is correct," Mr Shielding says looking impressed. "She has passed the first test. Most people when they are lying make up something that they think the raven would've said. We will try again." Shocked at this cruel trick I begin to glare at the tutor but the raven distracts me.

"Mr Shielding is the best tutor ever. His favourite food is pancakes and he likes to read." The raven says. Shocked I look at Mr Shielding and repeat what the bird said. Mr Shielding pauses and gives me an interested stare.

"She is telling us the truth," Mr Shielding says looking impressed. Mrs Steerly glares at me, her face twisted in fury.

"Just because she can talk to animals, doesn't mean she wasn't the one smashing and taking eggs. It's probably how she managed to capture the phoenix so easily," she says looking superior once again.

"The raven tells me that Amelia thinks it is Tom that took the phoenix. She saw him with a red egg out in the garden," Mr Shielding replies, looking at the two women sadly. I gasp in surprise. How did the raven know that? I wasn't thinking it and haven't thought about it in days. I've been too preoccupied with my magic and bonding with Azure.

"The boy that can camouflage?" Mrs Steerly asks looking

upset. The other's nod. "Bring him here. Amelia, you may go," she says reluctantly. Miss Clover holds me by the arm painfully as we leave the office, pulling me as fast as she can down the corridor. When we are nearly at the meal hall, I finally get the nerve to speak.

"How did the raven know about Tom?" I ask her confused. She begins to slow down, looking at me worriedly.

"A raven can read your mind, especially if you are trying to keep something a secret. That's why Mrs Steerly called for it, you would've been found a liar and anything else that you may have been hiding," she replies. "She will do the same to Tom and if your suspicions are correct..." I can see that she doesn't want to finish the sentence and I don't want her to either.

Miss Clover escorts me back to my room, where I check on Azure. He's sleeping soundly under his rock. I don't dare wake him, he's been through a rough day and probably needs his sleep. I'm too worried about Azure to concentrate on lessons for the rest of the day, so decide to skip them. I will have to ask my friends what I've missed. Laying comfortably on the bed, I think of Alice and the way she healed Azure. She really has impressive magic and she is clever. She really could be the next heir!

Chapter 11

I must drift off to sleep at some point as when I open my eyes again Alice and AJ are noisily entering the room.

"Oh, good you're back, but now they've taken Tom!" Alice exclaims looking worried. I feel guilty, they wouldn't have taken him if the raven hadn't have been able to read my thoughts. I tell them all about my time in the office and how I had seen Tom in the garden that day. The only thing I leave out is him possibly knowing a way to escape. Tears well up in my eyes as I start to cry, the guilt and emotions of the day have been too overwhelming for me to keep in any longer.

"It will be OK," AJ says, coming over and hugging me. "The raven will show them he is innocent and he will be let free."

Feeling a bit better, we go down to the evening meal with Azure firmly back on my wrist. Everyone is talking about Tom and I being taken and the phoenix being returned to its owner. Quietly, I sit and focus on my friends, trying hard not to let the voices consume me with dizziness.

Surprisingly we are awoken the next morning by a servant entering our room. This has never happened before so we don't know how to react. The sad and skinny girl enters, puts some clothes on the end of each of our beds and tells us to put them on. She then leaves. Looking at them, they are all black.

"This can't be good," I exclaim as we hurriedly pull them on.

Creatures are pocketed and wrapped around wrists as we are directed past the meal hall and out into the cold, crisp morning. Shivering we all walk to the open patch of grass. I look in horror as I realise what is happening. There, on a hastily built platform is Tom and Mrs Steerly. Tom has handcuffs around his hands and a heavy chain wrapped around his waist, his pixie by his side is also chained. Mrs Steerly looks like it's her birthday and someone has given her the greatest present she could've wished for.

All of the children and tutors stop and stand in front of the platform looking uneasily at each other. Mrs Steerly waits for us all to be quiet.

"Today, is a very sad day indeed, for we have an enemy in our group. This boy seemed to think that he could increase his chances of becoming the heir by murdering and capturing helpless creatures, thereby removing their owners from the competition. He is no friend to you and he is no friend to the Royal Family. Creatures are a valued and honoured companion and should not be harmed unless they or their owners have been dishonourable. The punishment for such a crime is death. Tom, you have been found guilty of your crimes and I will carry out your punishment."

I gasp horrified and bring my hands to my face trying to shield my eyes from what is about to happen. Tom has tears falling from his eyes, looking scared and frail. The boy that I have seen every spring for five years is broken and bruised. I have seen him deliver hundreds of lambs, he has cleaned up my grazed knees when I have fallen, I have seen him laugh and joke whilst having meals, looking carefree with so much life in him. He has been hardworking and was looked up to by many on the farm. He is about to be killed. I can't believe it.

Mrs Steerly grabs the pixie first and places her hand on its head. The pixie doesn't cry out in pain as it takes its last breath, the life taken from it, but Tom screams in agony. He is now openly sobbing and holding his chest like he has been stabbed through the heart, the pain of losing his creature is too much to bear. Mrs Steerly then throws the lifeless pixie to the floor like a useless rag and walks slowly to Tom. I want to look away but I can't. I owe him this much, for it was my doing that got him here as well as his own decisions. He didn't do the right thing in hurting creatures, not at all, but it was my suspicions that got him found out and so part of the blame is on me for him being on this platform this morning.

He has many more bruises than he came here with but the bruising from his eye that he got on the day we arrived here is still visible in the corners, the bruising turning yellow and green. The bruising that will now never heal. Mrs Steerly places her hand on Tom's head and it is as quick as lightning, he slumps to the floor.

All around there are muffled sobs and children crying

but I am numb with shock. I cannot process what I have just seen. It is too bad, too unbelievable to be true. Somehow, we all make it back to the meal hall, but no one eats anything. The day is spent doing our usual routine, but we are all sad, we are all quiet and we all follow the rules.

Chapter 12

"Why do you think he did it?" Alice asks, tears still pouring down her cheeks. Alice and I are back upstairs in our room. The day has been long and emotional, I can barely stand with the exhaustion that's consuming me.

I think about how Tom was when he was on the farm. He wasn't mean to anyone that I knew of. Why did he change so much when he arrived here? Slowly I get up and go down the corridor. I need to ask someone who might know, I am going to ask his friends.

I enter the green group's bedroom. Two boys and a girl are each sitting on their beds, they look just as tired and upset as we do. They look up as I enter, puzzled expressions on their faces.

"Can I come in? I knew Tom from back in the village, would it be OK if I came and talked to you about him? Just for a little bit?" I ask.

They look at each other uneasily and the girl nods. She is a few years older than me, probably around 15 with ginger hair and freckles smattering her nose and cheeks. A pixie is curled up asleep on her lap. The boys look around the same age, one has black hair and is holding a gnome, the other boy has brown hair and is holding some sort of lizard, I think it might be a gecko. I'm glad to see Alice has followed me, we both sit on the bed closest to the door. Instantly I can tell that I have done something wrong as each of the children tense as they watch me.

"Was this Tom's bed?" I ask sadly. Nobody says anything, but the girl nods again. "I'm Amelia and this is Alice, we both worked with Tom every spring. I guess we just don't understand. He was never mean and always so happy and helpful. We don't know why he would've done what he did. We were wondering if you had any ideas?"

I look around at their suspicious faces. I know they resent us being here but if they know anything then I need to hear it. It is quiet for a long time; I'm just about to give up and walk out when the black-haired boy in the bed next to me speaks.

"I'm Peter, this is Luke and Anna," he says nodding at each of them in turn. "He kept talking about his family. He had been the only one able to work, his father was crippled or something. He had a younger sister and he took care of her. Being taken... I mean sent here was hard on him. He kept going on and on about how he had to become the heir or try to escape. He seemed scared and frustrated a lot of the time."

I sit quietly as I try and process what I've heard. Maybe all of it did come down to fear and needing to save his family. I don't know how Caroline is coping without me, but I am glad that she is older, she wasn't dependant on me or my income. It must have been awful for Tom to feel trapped here and unable to help. Tom could have told the tutors I didn't have magic, but he didn't. That surely shows the good in him too. Thinking about that day I remember that he said something about there being a way to escape. He almost told me but we were interrupted.

"He talked about escaping…Did he tell you he knew of a way?" I ask quietly not wanting anyone else to overhear.

Anna pushes her pixie off her lap and goes to shut the door. The pixie gives me a bit of a disgruntled look as if it were my fault that it had been disturbed. I try and tell it 'Sorry' in my head. I think it works though as the pixie then gives me a little smile. Happy that I have communicated with the pixie without saying anything out loud, I then concentrate back on Anna.

"He said there was a wall… over near a vegetable patch and the kitchens. He thought none of the soldiers guarded just there but it was too high to get over. It helped that he could camouflage with his environment for a few seconds. If he could've done it for longer, I reckon he would have been gone long ago," Anna says looking crestfallen. "He wouldn't be dead now if he had". She starts to cry loudly then puts her head face down on the pillow muffling the sound.

Alice and I look at each other. I don't think there is anything else we can ask and we seem to have upset Anna enough to carry on.

"Thank you for talking to us," I say, as we walk out the door and back to our room.

"I don't think Tom was a bad guy," Alice says quietly.

"I don't either," I agree.

Chapter 13

The next few days we work hard on practising our magic and working with our creatures. I have a lot to catch up on as I had missed a few days of work. Once when I was dizzy and another time when I was in Mrs Steerly's office. We don't know what the assessments will entail or how we will be graded so everyone is tense and anxious.

At the evening meal the day before the assessments are to take place, Mrs Steerly comes in and stands on the platform. Everyone immediately quietens down. We haven't seen her since Tom's execution and I feel a mixture of sadness and anger as she stands before us.

"Tomorrow you will have your assessments. They will be taken by your tutor individually. I hope that you have been working hard up until now as after tomorrow we will all be expecting much more from you. Good luck," she smiles sweetly and leaves the room.

"Have you caught up with Etiquette Amelia?" Alice asks me nervously as she puts a forkful of pasta in her mouth.

"Yes, and History, I'm still not great at Business though. I don't think any amount of teaching will get me good at that," I reply unhappily looking at my food and feeling sick with nerves.

"I'm OK with my magic so I should be good there but all the rest confuses me. I don't know what fork I have to eat my salad with, why can't we just eat with the same one?" AJ sighs frustratedly.

"My magic is OK, but Dora and I don't have any idea what hers are yet. How are you two getting on with your creatures?" Alice says looking worriedly between us.

I look at Azure contentedly wrapped around my wrist. We have discussed this topic many times late into the night. I can now speak quite easily with him without making a sound so we don't disturb the others. We think Azure might have super strength, that's why he was able to open the door that day when we were rescuing the phoenix but we haven't been able to test it properly yet.

"Azure and I might have a bit of an idea but we could be wrong. We haven't got very far with it yet. What about you AJ?" I ask. He looks quite nervous, looking around hesitantly to see if anyone is listening, but everyone appears to be engrossed in their own conversations.

"I think he can transport himself to other places, he keeps disappearing and I find him in a different part of the room. You know he can't get around much on his own - having no legs and just a tail. It would be awesome if he did have that ability. Being water creatures they can share their magic with humans, I would be able to transport with him. Think of the places I could go!" He exclaims happily.

I don't dare say out loud what I am thinking, that if AJ is right then it really would be amazing. He could leave, he could escape from here. I wonder if that has occurred to him? Surely it has. I can't be the only one that thinks of leaving every minute of the day. Nodding slowly, I try to show my enthusiasm for his discovery but I can't help feeling jealous. AJ could be free.

The next day no one eats anything at breakfast. Our whole lives could be affected by what happens today. Miss Clover has told us that we will have our assessments at different times and will be tested on everything all at once.

"Apart from you Amelia, you will have your magic and creature bonding assessment with Mr Shielding. He's going to meet you at the stables after lunch," she instructs.

I look at her confused for a few seconds until I remember that Mr Shielding can also talk to animals, it will be easier for him to test my magic. Dread fills my body as I wonder what he will test me on. I've only known about my powers for a few weeks, what happens if he thinks they aren't good enough? I don't know him very well and I trust Miss Clover. I hoped that she was going to be as nice as she seemed. Mr Shielding could be really ruthless!

Each child's assessment lasts an hour. Damian is first, then AJ, then me and then Alice. Mine will be half an hour with Miss Clover then the rest with Mr Shielding. We wait for our names to be called in an almost empty room with just two lines of chairs. We don't talk much, although I can hear Alice muttering information under her breath over and over.

Damian looks his usual smug self as he comes into the room after his test and says AJ is next. He is not allowed to be in here, he is just supposed to call the next person and leave, free to do what he likes for the rest of the day. He'll be in trouble if anyone finds him here, he could be telling us the questions and answers in advance, giving us all help. This is Damian though and he wouldn't help us if our lives depended on it. He just sits down and continues to look smug making us more nervous.

"I found it easy but I doubt that you will Amelia, bet you don't even know who your parents are let alone the Royal Family lines, and Business... get real, you'd probably die of shock if you had enough money to buy yourself more than two bags of rice. Why don't you just give up now and leave? The servants wear brown, don't they? It would really suit you!" He teases as he pets his merturtle.

"Go away, Damian!" I say through gritted teeth, trying to keep calm. I look at his merturtle, Melvin and lock eyes with him. I don't mean to, but I am not in control of my emotions. I am too nervous about the test and too frustrated and angry with Damian's behaviour towards me. "You should slap his hand away with your tail, make him feel bad for being mean," I think to Melvin. Everyone stares in shock as the merturtle jumps jerkily up, slaps Damian and rolls off his lap. Damian jumps up enraged. Fortunately, he doesn't know that I can talk to the animals without speaking out loud, so to him, it looks like Melvin has just acted crazy.

Alice and I can't hide our smirks as Damian strides out of the room angry and humiliated, carrying his merturtle loosely in one hand. I suddenly feel bad as I realise that Damian will take his anger out on Melvin; he won't know it was me. I am confused though, I only told it what to do, he didn't have to do it...did he? I think this over for a few minutes. Maybe he wanted to do it, Damian must be a horrible person to have around all of the time. I go back to trying to remember the Royal Family line...maybe Damian did me a favour by being here after all. He may have given me a clue as to what was on the test. AJ returns and tells me it is my turn.

"Good luck!" Alice wishes me as I go through the door. Azure gives my wrist a small squeeze for comfort.

I knock on the door and enter the assessment room. Miss Clover is sitting at the table and gestures to a seat in front of her. As I am about to sit, I notice something out of the corner of my eye, turning around I am astonished to see it is Mrs Steerly. She is sitting in the back corner looking happy and relaxed. I stop dead when I see her, my heart pounding even more wildly in my chest. I almost blurt out demanding to know what she is doing here but just in time, I stop myself. I would've earned zero points in etiquette if I had uttered a word. I stagger towards the chair and sit down heavily, feeling her gaze prickle the back of my head.

"Right Amelia, let's start, shall we?" Mrs Clover says, her voice as tense as every muscle in my body. I can't think why Mrs Steerly is here, why isn't she watching anyone else's tests, why did she have to come to mine? I blink rapidly and try to focus, Mrs Clover is setting out a plate, knives, spoons and forks.

"Can you tell me which fork is used for which part of the meal, please?" She asks.

I am about to point to the one on the outside and work inwards but I have noticed that Miss Clover has switched the two middles ones so they are in the wrong place. I look at her wondering if she has noticed her error but she is just looking at me encouragingly. Could this be a part of the test? Does Miss Clover know her error, or am I mistaken? I lick my lips with uncertainty.

"Miss Clover, the two middle forks are in the wrong place, the slightly shorter one should be further out," I say, pointing to the forks and shaking with nerves.

I hear Mrs Steerly's hum of disapproval behind me but don't dare to turn round. My heart sinks as I realise I must have been incorrect judging by her reaction. Miss Clover then switches the forks and writes something down on her notepad that is hidden out of view. My palms sweat as I tell her my answers. Next I'm asked about the correct greetings and manners in different situations, but to my horror, she asks me to do a curtsy.

"Just like you would if you were meeting the Queen," Miss Clover says, a smile on her face. This is one of the first things they taught us and practised on many occasions so you would think that I would be good at it by now. Unfortunately, I am not very graceful. I grew up doing manual jobs, there was no need to do things delicately. Taking a deep breath, I put one foot forward and bend my other knee, sweeping my arms out to the side and bending my back until i'm looking at the floor. I try not to wobble on the way down, but I know my arm wavers as I start to lose my balance. Without being told to, I return to standing. I think it's better to get out of the curtsy early than to fall flat on my face in front of Mrs Steerly. Thankfully, nothing is said about my early finish, but Miss Clover does write more down on her notepad.

We move on to History, I recite what I have learned about the family line. Starting at the latest and working back. I mention poor dead Prince Austin feeling uncomfortable. Then there's Queen Harriet and King Phillip. King Phillip's mother and father were Emma and Alexander and on and on I go, only giving out the line of succession. We are never taught about the rest of the family or if there are any other brothers or sisters, cousins or any other relations. I remember hearing that one queen had five children, but no one knows the names of the other four, they don't seem to matter. The only important line is the one that becomes a king or queen. As they are royalty they all have the right to own creatures. Thinking about it, I wonder what those creatures were and how many there are living in the castle now.

The Business test is quite tricky, I am given a scenario of which kingdom it would be better to trade with, one that has gold and silks but has a king that charges too much or the other which has exotic foods and jewels but our relationship with him is strained and unpleasant. I also have to give my reasons for which I pick and why I didn't choose the other. Picking the last one, I hope that trading with the kingdom will bond us together.

"That is us finished Amelia, don't forget to see Mr Shielding later," Miss Clover says smiling brightly at me as she opens the door. "Please send Alice in." I walk towards the room where Alice has been waiting and tell her she can go in and good luck. She smiles at me nervously.

"I think you did well," Azure says to me proudly.

"Thank you, I hope so. It really made me worried when I saw Mrs Steerly," I reply. "I hope she isn't there when I am with Mr Shielding, I will be anxious enough as it is. Are you ready for us to perform?" I ask teasingly, for Azure will be being tested as much as I will in the next half of the assessment.

Chapter 14

We walk in the gardens together before lunch, the sun is warm and there is only a light refreshing breeze. Azure decides to slither along next to me. The other children back away slightly when they see us, still a little scared from the memory of him attacking anyone that came near me when I was unconscious on the floor.

After lunch, I head to the stables to meet Mr Shielding, leaving Alice and AJ happily walking in the gardens to enjoy the warm weather. For them their assessment is over, I still have half of mine left.

Reaching the stables, I see Mr Shielding is already there waiting, stroking the black horse with a white nose that I have become fond of. Fortunately, Mrs Steerly is nowhere to be seen.

"Good afternoon Mr Shielding," I say pleasantly, hoping that if I am nice then he won't be too hard on me.

"Good afternoon, Amelia," he replies, smiling. I hadn't noticed before but he has dimples in his cheek similar to Caroline and I. This instantly makes me warm to him as he feels like home.

"I have already seen some of your abilities, so we will make this quick," he says reaching into his jacket and pulling out the scruffy-looking raven again.

"I would like you to make this raven do a little trick, anything that comes to mind but I don't want you to say it out loud, do you think you can do that?" He asks me, looking hopeful.

"Erm... Yes OK, I'll try," I reply frantically trying to think of something I can make the bird do. Firstly, I look at the bird and try to stare into its eyes, his eyes are similar to Azure's but they aren't quite as calm looking, seeming a little scared.

"Raven, fly into the air and do a loop, then come and sit on my shoulder," I think to it screwing up my face in concentration. I wait a few seconds but the bird doesn't move. Just when I'm about to try again it opens its wings and flaps. It takes a little bit more effort than I imagined but the raven flies up and round in a circle. It then comes and sits on my shoulder.

"Ouch!" I cry as the raven nips at my ear. "What was that for?" I ask it out loud.

"I'm fifty-six years old! How would you like it if I told you to fly around like that at my age? My wings make creaking noises if I do too much. I'll be in agony for days!" It complains to me.

"You didn't have to do it if you didn't want to. I would've thought of something else," I tell it feeling guilty.

"Didn't I?" He replies not sounding convinced. Our conversation is interrupted by Mr Shielding clapping.

"Well done Amelia, that was great work. Sorry about Felix here, not the most agile of creatures now," he apologises as he comes over, reaching a hand out for the bird to hop back onto. "The next test will be for you and your creature. Please place him on the floor for me, between the two of us," he says, putting poor Felix back into his jacket pocket. I tell Azure what to do, so he slithers from my wrist and onto the floor.

Before I have time to process what is going on, Mr Shielding pulls back his jacket and reveals a long sword, he grabs its handle and pulls it out from its holder brandishing it menacingly at me. Azure instantly raises his head in an attack position; ready to strike.

"What are you doing?" I cry out, unsure if he is really about to kill me. My brain catches up and I realise that it must be part of the test as it would've been easier to harm me with Azure on my wrist.

Azure is weaving side to side, his venomous sharp fangs directed at the tutor. Mr Shielding takes a swing at him with the sword, only narrowly missing Azure's neck. The snake then retaliates by lunging swiftly at him, catching him on the sleeve. I don't dare breathe as I watch them fight but just as suddenly as it started, Mr Shielding stops and drops the sword. For a moment I wonder if he has been seriously hurt, did Azure's fangs dig into him? Have we killed a tutor? My mind rushes with explanations and excuses as to how this happened, wondering if anyone will believe it was an accident. I look at the tutor and expect him to fall to the ground but instead he is smiling again, showing his dimples.

"Well done! You passed!" He says excitedly. "You are doing very well together," he nods looking proudly at us both.

Azure sinks down but doesn't take his eyes off of the tutor, ready for any other unexpected attacks. My breathing and heart rate slow down as I realise the threat is over but I'm not happy with Mr Shielding at all. Did he have to be so dramatic?

"Sorry about that but I had to be sure," he says looking guilty. "Come and meet the horses, I believe you already know Domino," he says going over to the black and white one again. The horses are still calm and content, the activity of the false attack not having affected them at all. I try and calmly walk over towards the horse and stroke its neck, very aware of the tutor beside me.

"What did you used to do... before?" He asks me interestedly.

It takes me a while to answer, the memories of the farm and home washing over me. How even though Caroline hated me, she would still look after me the best she could. When I was sick, she would always give me her share of the meal. There were little things that I had forgotten and now that I wasn't there anymore, they were the things I missed.

"Most of the time I either worked with the Blacksmith or at the farm with the sheep," I answer, trying not to sound upset, wishing I was back home.

"Ah, sheep, not the most communicative of animals. Probably for the best though. I never like talking to an animal and then realising it's going to be for someone's meal," he says bluntly.

"I hadn't thought of that! Hey, sheep it's been nice talking to you but I really fancy some stew tonight and you're on the menu!" I laugh out loud, releasing the tension I had been holding onto all day.

Mr Shielding laughs along with me as we both pet Domino. Azure joins me by wrapping himself around my waist like a belt, apparently happy that the tutor is no longer a threat.

"We'd better go, but I am requesting that you take Magic and Creature bonding with me from now on. As we both have the same abilities, I will be able to teach you more effectively. Unfortunately, this does mean that I will teach you in the evening for an hour. Your first class will now be Etiquette meaning you have most of the morning off. I'll meet you tomorrow here at the stables, an hour before the evening meal," Mr Shielding says as we walk back towards the building together.

Chapter 15

The next day there are regular lessons in the morning but after lunch, we all have to meet outside on the grass for an announcement. We are guessing it's about the results of our assessments. Waving at Alice and AJ as they walk off to Creature bonding and Magic, Azure and I head outside. Whilst everyone is busy with their lessons, I think it would be a good opportunity to look for the part of the wall that Anna mentioned. Tom had told them that it was near the kitchens but I had never been that way before, so I wandered across the wide patch of grass where I thought it could be.

The day is cloudy with a slight chill as I walk across the grass, it is a long time before I get to the back of the building where I think the kitchens are but, on the way, I notice that there is a large vegetable patch. Anna mentioned this would be roughly the right place. I look around for any soldiers and walk closer.

There are still a few trees surrounding the grounds but I see that there is a high wall cutting through them continuing to surround the building, this must be where Tom meant. The trees thin out near the wall and there is a small space, where someone could hide. As long as a soldier wasn't looking directly at them, they could be concealed in a few seconds. There's still the problem of getting over the wall. Looking around at the trees, none have low enough branches to climb up. I'm so focused on looking for an escape that I don't hear the voices coming closer at first. Panicking I look behind me, I don't want anyone to see me lurking here. Mrs Steerly is heading towards me with a man I don't recognise. If this is going to be a way of escape, she mustn't get suspicious. I look around but there is nowhere else to hide except that small space I have just found between the trees and the wall - the place that I don't know if it's safe to enter without being shot by a soldier! Taking a deep breath, I realise it's my only choice and dash into the gap. No fires are shot or yells are heard as I wait crouched in the trees. Mrs Steerly's voice gets louder as she passes my hiding place.

"They must be removed quickly with as little fuss as possible," she says with urgency. I wait for a few minutes after I am certain that she has gone out of sight and creep out again. I shiftily look around making sure I am alone, before hurrying back the way I came.

"I think we've found it!" I say to Azure excitedly. "There's the little problem of finding a way over the wall but I'm sure we will manage it somehow. I'm just glad we didn't get shot!"

"I'm very glad we didn't get shot either!" Replies Azure. "It does look a good place and very well hidden." We both laugh nervously together, elated to have discovered something that gives me hope.

Later, all of us stand outside on the grass waiting for Mrs

Steerly's announcement. I haven't had the chance to tell Alice and AJ about the wall near the kitchens that I had discovered. I'm so excited, I'm finding it difficult not to tell them what I have found but we need to be alone. With a bit of thought, we could all be free.

We all stand quietly as Mrs Steerly comes across the grass towards the platform where Tom was killed. A wave of sickness washes over me as I look at the spot where he stood. Determindly, I try and force the images of that day out of my head so I can concentrate on what is being said. I wish Azure was in his usual place wrapped around my wrist, but we were all told to leave our creatures in our rooms. Mrs Steerly arrives, followed by four men who are each holding a small box.

"What's with the scary-looking men?" Alice leans towards me and whispers in my ear.

"I don't know, I saw one of them talking to Mrs Steerly earlier, she said something about not making a fuss. What do you think is in those boxes?" I whisper back.

Before we can continue our conversation, AJ nudges me painfully in the side. He scowls at us and hurridly returns his gaze to the platform. Looking forward, I realise Mrs Steerly is giving us a murderous glare. I bow my head apologetically, hoping that I won't be in trouble later.

"As I was saying," Mrs Steerly shouts out in her clear and crisp voice. "Most of you have done surprisingly well in the assessments. So we have decided to give some of you a little prize to award you for your hard work. Could Liam, Damian, Anna, and Andrew come and stand to my right and Ben, Claire, Olivia and Luke please come and stand on my left."

There is a lot of movement and shuffling around as the eight children go to their places on stage. I am annoyed to see Damian up there, he looks arrogantly down at us on the grass below him.

"Liam, for your hard work, Well done," Mrs Steerly congratulates him as one of the men steps forward and gives Liam the small box. Mrs Steerly continues to congratulate the remaining three children on her right, giving each of them a box. We all clap as each box is received. Mrs Steerly then looks to her left, where the other four children are waiting. The men are standing behind them. I look on puzzled. There aren't any more boxes to give out. Suddenly, each of the men grabs a child tightly and forces them off stage.

"What's going on?" Luke yells as he is dragged away. I recognise him from the green group. He was the brown-haired boy with the gecko I talked to about Tom. I take a small step forward, I'm unsure why, maybe to try and help him but AJ grabs hold of my tunic and pulls me back. Annoyed, I look at him as he shakes his head. Helplessness settles over me. What did I think I was going to do, run and help him? That will get me sent to the same place he is going. I stare back at Mrs Steerly angrily. That was a cruel trick, they thought they were there to be rewarded but were taken instead. It was so quick and simple. So clever. The four children that are left on the platform are looking around uneasily, probably unsure if they are next.

"Unfortunately, four children have had to leave us. Their marks on the assessment were poor and they would not have been suitable to be the next heir," Mrs Steerly says, trying to look sad at their departure but we all know better. She is probably fighting to hide a smile. "You may all return to your scheduled lesson."

We all head towards our History class too shocked to speak. Mr Shielding is waiting for us, a sombre look on his face. From a class of nine there are now only six of us and only two are left from white group. Damian is the only one of us that looks even the slightest bit happy.

Before the evening meal, I head to the stables to have my lesson with Mr Shielding. I'm glad I have the opportunity to escape as Damian was even more smug than usual. In the box was a golden badge. If we had taken it back to my village, we could have sold it to feed half the families for a year. He had walked around the room with it pinned to his tunic stopping at each of our beds and asking us how it looked. It had taken a lot of comforting words from Azure for me not to slap him.

I get to the stables and find them empty, so take the opportunity to give all the horses a sugar lump, trying hard to block out their voices as they all beg for one at the same time. I stroke Domino's nose and tell him how handsome he is. The horse doesn't speak the same as Azure does to me, there are only single words or a few together making a small sentence. You can't really have a conversation, but it's nice to hear what he has to say. I still can't believe that I can hear him at all. It is such a great gift to have. Mr Shielding enters the barn and comes across to Domino, Azure and me.

"You seem to have quite a bond with each other," he says gesturing to the horse. I smile fondly at Domino and pat him on the nose.

"Well, he was the first animal I ever spoke to, at first I did think I was ill or going mad but I will always remember it," I reply.

"The first animal I ever talked to was a horse too. I used to sneak out of here riding one and go down to some of the villages. They always fascinated me, although it was hard to see so much suffering. I used to bring food to some of the families when I could," he says looking like he is thinking fondly of the past. "One time I almost got caught, there were soldiers around the gate I used so I had to find another way...There was a wall by the kitchens that is hidden from the soldiers."

I panic, my heart beating madly. Did someone see me this morning looking around and told the tutor? I stop breathing as I realise the punishment this could cause.

"Don't look so scared Amelia, I told Tom about it too, unfortunately, he didn't find a way to use it in time..." He says sadly.

"Why did you tell him?" I ask curiously, shocked at what I am hearing.

"I knew that he was the one destroying the eggs. A raven can read minds so Felix informed me. I told Tom about the wall so he could try and escape," he replies. I look at him puzzled, something stirring in the back of my mind. Shocked, I gasp out loud as I remember.

"But... But you told Mrs Steerly it was Tom when I was in her office... you were the reason he was found out!" I say accusingly. Mr Shielding pauses and looks crestfallen, taking a deep breath before he answers.

"It was either you or him and I had to pick you," he says simply.

My mind buzzes with what I have just heard. I can't understand it. Mr Shielding told Tom about the wall hoping he'd escape but then because I was in danger he then told on Tom... I look at Mr Shielding, he looks sad and apologetic but I can't process anything else right now. I run past him and out of the barn to the building, forgetting the lesson I am supposed to be having. He calls after me but I keep going.

I run until I am safely back in my room. I barge inside, startling AJ, Alice and Damian. Seeing Damian, I realise I can't talk in front of him, but I need to talk now and somewhere safely.

"Alice...AJ... can you come with me, I need to talk to you," I say as calmly as I can.

AJ and Alice get up and follow me, bringing their creatures. I head down the corridor and knock on the green rooms door, then walk in uninvited. Alice and AJ walk in and sit on Tom's old bed looking confused.

"What are you doing in here?" Peter demands looking at Anna for answers. Anna just shrugs and looks at us all.

I pace around the room in a frenzy, thoughts rattling around in my head that won't fit together. I tell them about my conversation with Mr Shielding. When I have finished, they all look as shocked as I feel, their mouths open wide.

"We have to escape... we have to find a way over the wall. Tom's dead, more have been taken. Who else is next?" I ask them, trying desperately to get them to help and agree to come with me. "We will have our creatures taken away from us, forced to be servants. We've all seen them as they bring us our meals, they look half-starved and exhausted. Some with black eyes or bruised faces. Do we really want to end up like that?" I cry.

"Before today I would've told you that you were mad, just like Tom but there are only two of us greens left and seeing them take Luke... It makes it seem so much more real. I will help you; I'll go with you. We need to find Tom's family, we need to help them. We need to do this for him," Peter says standing up, looking determined.

"I will too," says AJ standing up next to Peter.

"Me too," says Alice joining in. "I couldn't bear to be without Dora now." Anna looks down thoughtfully, her fingers feeling the golden badge pinned to her tunic.

110

"I will help you, but I don't know if I'll come. I may have a chance, don't you see... I may have a chance to be the next heir. Then I might be able to change things...I might be able to change the kingdom," she says, looking at all of us pleadingly.

I'm about to argue, about to tell her that she doesn't have much of a chance but how can I? I don't even know what magic she has. If she can become the heir and change the kingdom, who am I to stop her?

"That's your choice," I tell her and look to the rest of the group. "Does anyone have any ideas?" We talk after the evening meal and long into the night, but none of us can come up with a practical plan.

"We have to go, the tutors will be here to check on us soon," I say regretfully opening the door and letting AJ and Alice walk through before me.

"Wait!" Anna says rushing up to me. "I know you are mad at Mr Shielding but he did try and save Tom, even though he was hurting the creatures and then he did try to save you... that does count for something. What I want to know is... Why did he save your life over Tom's?" She asks, screwing up her face in thought.

"I don't know," I reply equally as confused.

"Maybe you need to find out?" She replies and shuts the door leaving me outside in the empty corridor.

Chapter 16

"Should I just ask him?" I ask Azure for the hundredth time as I am walking towards the stables for my next lesson with Mr Shielding. "Just come out and ask him why he chose to save me and not Tom?" I hear a big sigh in my head. AJ and Alice are both frustrated with me asking this same question and now Azure is fed up with me too.

"It might be a good idea but just remember that he might not tell you, or he might not tell you the truth," Azure replies with the same answer he has given to me also for the hundredth time.

"I'm finding you just as frustrating as you are finding me right now!" I complain at him and yank open the barn door. I'm shocked when I see Domino out of his stall with a harness and saddle on with Mr Shielding standing by his side.

"Ah, there you are Amelia!" He says joyfully, as though yesterday's conversation hadn't happened. "It's time for your riding lesson but obviously we will be doing things a bit differently from everyone else. You will be commanding the horse by using your abilities - no talking allowed!" He says grinning at me. I see the dimple in the side of his cheek and all my anger and nervousness disappears. I make a vow to myself that I will see Caroline's smile again.

"I've never ridden a horse before," I say reluctantly as I stand beside the tutor. Looking at the saddle I find somewhere to hold on to and place my foot in the stirrups, just like I've seen being done back at the farm and the blacksmiths. I try and hoist myself up, with my leg going over the horse's back but I soon find out that it is a lot harder than it looks. Frustratedly, I attempt it again and again. The fourth time I just about manage to get my leg over and pull myself up.

"What now?" I ask Mr Shielding rather breathless from the effort.

"Now command him, go wherever you like, I will follow behind," he responds.

Using my magic, I ask Domino to go forward slowly. The movement jerks me backwards and we walk across the field, Mr Shielding by my side. We walk in silence but I am anxiously trying to get the courage to ask him why he saved me and not Tom.

"I believe you have something to ask me?" Mr Shielding says. Surprised I look at him.

"Oh... Felix told you?" I realise. I think for a few moments. He already knows what I need to ask him but he is still making me say it. Irritated, I ask the question that has been haunting me all day. "Why me and not Tom?"

"I won't lie to you; I promise, but what I am about to say might shock you," he replies looking uneasy. "I knew your mother."

"What!" I shout confused. "How, When?"

"I knew her mostly all her life, I would come to visit her as often as I could until just before your sister Caroline was born. I was then unfortunately unable to do so. I couldn't have let you die, not being... not being her daughter..." He answers sadly. I am so shocked that I don't know what to say. He knew about me? He knew about Caroline? "One day I will tell you the whole story but not now. First, we have to get to know each other and I must help you with your magic. For you must be the next heir."

It is only when I am back in the green group's room relating what Mr Shielding has told me to Alice, AJ, Anna and Peter that it occurs to me that he has told me a way to escape but also told me that I must be the next heir.

"I'm so confused!" I shout out trying to make sense of the situation. "Which should I do? I don't think I'm good enough at my magic to be the heir and I hate all the lessons, being royal sounds mind-numbingly dull!"

"Being heir means you could change how the kingdom is run," Anna says forcefully.

"And you get to keep Azure," Alice chimes in.

"And be rich and eat mountains of food," AJ says enthusiastically.

"Or you could fail miserably and live your life as a servant just because some mad tutor has got some wild idea in his head," Peter concludes. We all look at Peter in horror. "Sorry, but it could happen!" He says guiltily.

"If you don't want to be heir then don't, just escape. I want to do it because I know that I can change this kingdom for the better. What I don't understand is, why does he think you should be the next heir instead of any of us?" Anna asks accusingly.

"I guess because he knew my mother," I reply feebly. "There isn't a reason why it should be me."

"OK, this is getting us nowhere. We need to think about the escape plan. You don't have to make up your mind now," Peter says.

"When do we go?" AJ asks, looking at us all.

"We need to find a way over the wall yet," I say frustrated as we still don't have a plan.

"If we manage to get out of the grounds, we need to be fast, it took us hours to get here by truck," Peter says, his head in his hands with exhaustion. "They'll know we are missing after a few hours if we go during the day, if we go at night then we have to navigate our way to the village in the darkness which will slow us down. We need to get somewhere we know well and hide."

"I don't suppose anyone has any magic that can make them go faster, do they?" Anna asks doubtfully.

"What about your merturtle, AJ? Can't he transport himself?" Alice asks excitedly. We all perk up; this could be the answer to the whole problem. Rio can just transport us out!

"No, he can only transport to where he has been before and we haven't managed to work out how he can give the ability to me yet," AJ says sadly.

"OK, well, keep working on it AJ...What magic do we and our creatures have?" I ask hopefully "Maybe we can find something that can work. I can talk to animals and I'm pretty sure Azure has super strength but I'm not sure how that's going to be any help."

"I can heal but that's only any use if one of us gets hurt. I'm still unsure what Dora can do, sorry," Alice says apologetically. Peter looks shiftily around and gives a big sigh.

"Look. I know this sounds bad but I promise that I don't use it for anything awful," he says looking worried. "But I can... I can put a thought into someone's mind and they think that it's their idea."

"Like mind control?" AJ asks shocked. We all look at Peter horrified. I try to think of a time that I have done something I wouldn't usually do but I can't think of anything.

"Eugh... I knew you'd take it this way - Everyone does," Peter says exasperated. "It's not as bad as you think. I don't think I could make someone kill themselves or anything, but I can make them go in a different direction thinking that they have forgotten something. It's only small, little things."

"For now... what happens when your magic gets stronger?" AJ says nervously.

116

"I know Peter, he wouldn't do anything like that. I trust him," Anna says sincerely.

"Then we trust him too," Alice says, trying to sound confident. The rest of us nod although AJ doesn't look quite so convinced.

"It could be useful anyway, making a soldier look the other way or something. Think of the possibilities," Anna says convincingly.

"So, what can you do then? You got an award so it must be pretty impressive," AJ asks looking peeved at Anna.

Anna closes her eyes and stays perfectly still for a few moments, then her features start to blur, her frizzy ginger hair turns black and coils into a bun. Her features merge together until, sitting before us, is the severe-looking image of Mrs Steerly!

"Oh, no, no, no!" Alice says as her face turns white with shock. It only lasts for a few more seconds and then Anna turns back into herself again, looking incredibly pleased.

"I can't do it for very long, only about a minute and I haven't got the voice right yet but it's quite awesome, isn't it?" Anna says boastfully. The rest of us nod silently, too shocked to speak.

"Between us, I think we all make a good team," Peter says looking hopeful.

"That could be very useful," I admit.

"Just me next and my pitiful ability to make things lighter. It doesn't seem at all impressive next to that!" AJ says sounding disheartened.

"Actually..." Anna says looking thoughtful. "That's perfect! Can't you just make us all really light so that you could carry us over the wall?" We all look at AJ enthusiastically. His eyes are bugging out of his head as he nods his head frantically.

"Yes!" He says gleefully, "Yes I could do that!"

"Fantastic, now all we have to do is find a way to get to the village quickly and when it would be the best time to go - then we should be OK!" Peter says, looking happier than I have ever seen him.

Chapter 17

We all work together discussing the plan over the coming days, trying to think of any detail we have missed or any problems that might occur. Alice, AJ and I spend most of our free time in the green group's room. Peter and Anna becoming our good friends. We enjoy challenging Anna's magic, making her turn into all the tutors and other children.

"Just think what you could do if you turned into the Queen!" AJ says laughing.

"I won't have to turn into her, I will become the heir and then I will be the real queen," she says confidently.

"You have to admire her determination," I say as we all head back to our room later that evening. "She knows what she wants and I wouldn't stand in her way." As we open the door, we see Damian is waiting for us, laying on his bed.

"Where do you lot keep going?" He asks accusingly.

"What... We aren't allowed to make other friends?" I say annoyed

"Aaaaw, I think our little Damainy is starting to miss our company," AJ teases.

"Oh, shut up! Hardly. I wish you would all stay there. I quite fancy the room to myself," he says, looking miffed.

"Don't worry Damian, we all agree that we'd rather be anywhere else than stuck with you," Alice says smugly. Damian looks furiously at us as we all get ready for bed. I feel victorious as I slip under the covers. We are no longer afraid of Damian. Together, we won.

"Be careful..." Azure says sleepily. "Don't get too cocky, I don't think Damian is a good enemy to have." I roll my eyes in the dark,

"Don't ruin my mood!" I say irritated.

The next day at breakfast Mr Shielding comes into the meal hall and looks around, stopping when he sees me. Usually, we only see tutors for classes so his appearance makes me anxious.

"I need to see you right now, Amelia," he says gruffly, worry etched on his face in deep lines. I stand up quickly, leaving my unfinished porridge on the table. Alice and AJ's concerned faces look at me as I head out of the door behind the tutor. I can't think of anything that I have done - except try and escape and Mr Shielding was the one that told me how. Unless another tutor has worked out what is going on... I look at Mr Shielding's back as he hurries us to the stables. When I am inside he shuts the door and turns around looking panicked.

"There's going to be an attack on your village tomorrow! Have you and your friends found a way to escape?" He asks hurriedly. I try to process what he is saying but I am too alarmed to get past the first sentence.

"They are going to attack the village?" I question. Surely, I couldn't have heard right. Why would they do such a thing?

"Yes!" Mr Shielding replies agitatedly "They have decided to take or kill anyone that might be using magic... which as you know is practically all of them. Your friends must go and warn them, they must escape today!"

"I have to go warn Caroline, she might be in danger!" I cry looking at the tutor in fright.

"No, only your friends must go. You must stay here and try to become the heir; promise me you will stay!" He commands. I shake my head in confusion.

"Why must I stay? I could be free, why don't you want that for me too?" I shout forcefully.

"Shh. Quiet, we'll be heard. I promise I will tell you the reason you must stay and become the heir soon but right now we urgently have to warn the people of the village. Make sure Alice goes, she can heal anyone that's hurt. Now quickly, tell me the plan," he orders. Dismayed I realise that we haven't actually got a working plan. We only know that we were going to go at night and how we were going to get over the wall. I tell him the plan so far.

"Take Domino, explain to him what the plan is now and the urgency to stay quiet. He will obey you. They can all ride him to the village and hopefully warn everyone in time. I must get back, try and act as normally as possible. We don't want anyone suspecting anything. Be careful," he says giving my arm a small squeeze of comfort before he rushes off out the door.

I quickly tell Domino the plan, trying to recall every detail that had been discussed.

"Honoured to serve," he says to me after I have finished. I give him a quick sugar lump and head back to my room. Fortunately, my lessons don't start until late morning so there's still time to go over everything and think of anything that I have missed.

Frustratingly, I am unable to tell my friends what Mr Shielding said until lunch and it is only a quick conversation to prepare them for tonight and tell them they are taking Domino.

"But we haven't found out where the soldiers guard at night or anything yet. We aren't ready!" AJ says panicking.

"We will just have to work around anything we find," I say tensely. "Just act normally," I stress to each of them as we head to afternoon classes. Fortunately, Peter and Anna are in a different class than the rest of us, otherwise, I'm sure the tutors would suspect something is wrong.

Mr Shielding appears calm as he takes the class, I wonder if he will still make me come to our private lesson. He waits until the class is empty before he calls me over.

"When you come to the lesson later, we can discuss any issues. I would say to cancel it but it's important we keep to the schedule so as not to attract any attention," he says. I nod my head and leave, joining my friends upstairs in the green group's room.

"Are there any problems that anyone can think of that Mr Shielding might be able to help with?" I ask them all hurriedly before I head down to the lesson.

"Oh, only about a hundred things could go wrong," AJ says struggling to keep calm. "There may be soldiers everywhere, we could get lost on the way to the village and none of us knows how to ride a horse... Just to name a few."

"Domino is taking you, all you have to do is hold on tightly to him and each other," I say, hoping to sound reassuring as I leave for the stables.

"Am I mad to be trying to attempt this?" I ask Azure as I hurry down the corridor.

"Oh yes, definitely," he replies.

"Thanks for your support," I say, rolling my eyes at him even though he can't see it.

I repeat the plan three times to Mr Shielding and we work through the problems together.

"The tutors do a last check that everyone is in bed at midnight," Mr Shielding explains. "They then go to their rooms which are all near the kitchens, so don't make any noise over that side. The soldiers are usually on the roof, but some do come down to the gardens at around 2am and 4am to stretch their legs and look around. It's best to go before 2am so you can get to the village in time. The attack is supposed to happen in the morning. Good luck."

After the evening meal, I tell everyone the latest details. They all look scared and anxious.

"I think we should try and sleep now," I say to them all. "It will be a long and stressful night for all of us, you travelling and alerting the village and the rest of us worrying about you. We should all sleep in here but Rio and Azure need to go back to the tank. I know we need to do things as normally as possible but we may need help. Everyone will need rest."

I tell Rio and Azure the plan. Alice looks relieved that she won't have to be parted from Dora. We all settle on the beds and close our eyes. There is a lot of tossing and turning and I don't think any of us sleep but we do get some rest. After a few hours AJ, Alice and I head back to our room, pretending that all we've been doing is having our usual chat with our friends. I try desperately to look happy and carefree but I know I fail miserably. Azure and Rio look happy in the tank and Damian is already asleep as we go in and lie down.

"How has Damian been, Azure? Do you think he suspects anything?" I ask him in my head. "Not that I noticed although he's been asleep for a while," he answers sleepily.

I settle into bed but this time I must not fall asleep. We have to be up soon. The escape is about to happen.

Chapter 18

Azure and I creep out after I am sure that the tutors have checked all of our rooms. The corridor is dark as I walk as softly as I can, trying not to scuff my feet on the stone floor. All around me is eerily quiet, the only thing I can hear is my heart pounding loudly in my ears. I reach the door to the lane and try to open it as silently as I can but it doesn't move.

"The door's locked!" I scream in my head to Azure. "Why didn't Mr Shielding warn us that they lock the doors at night?"

I am so frustrated and upset I can't think. What are we going to do? We don't have time to try all the doors. The others are to meet us here in a few minutes after I've retrieved Domino.

"We could work together and use our strength," Azure says to me.

"You're a genius!" I reply. "But we have to try and be as quiet as possible. Can you manage without hissing?"

"Our powers work better if I do but we can try without it first," he replies determinedly.

I take a deep breath and pull as hard as I can. Azure makes a faint glow but it is clear that we won't be able to open it. I feel like crying over our failure.

"Let's try again but with the hiss, if we don't open this door then we are in deep trouble," I say to Azure. I pull as hard as I can, my arms straining and my muscles hurting. Azure starts to hiss softly, trying to be as quiet as he can but it still won't open. He glows blue and his hissing gets louder. I think I can start to hear it echoing throughout the corridor. Azure continues to glow brighter and brighter. I hope there are no soldiers around as we are lighting up the corridor like the sun!

Finally, I feel the door budge, but there is a scraping of metal so loud that we may have just screamed at the top of our voices that we were here! Hurriedly, I try and close the door again, but the metal has twisted so much that it doesn't shut properly. Outside, my eyes try and adjust to the sudden blackness. I'm hoping that I can find my way to the stables but everything looks so different in the dark. I can only see a short distance in front of me, I carefully move forward trying not to trip over on the uneven ground. Listening around me, I try to hear if any soldiers are heading my way, but all is quiet with only the sound of the wind rustling through the trees.

My heart is pounding with nerves as I get to the stables and I am breathless with anxiety, but fortunately, I don't need to use my voice as I instruct Domino on what to do.

"It's a good job you are black, you might not be seen in the dark," I tell Domino as he plods along beside me on the grass. "Azure, go and find the others, hopefully, they will follow you to the wall. We can't stay here, we made too much noise getting out," I order him. He unwraps himself from around my wrist and slithers off into the night.

We have to take a longer route around the garden, so we don't step on any stone as Domino's hooves slap loudly on the ground. This means going very close to the treeline and this scares me most of all. Soldiers will expect anyone escaping to go through the trees. Unbelievably I don't think any soldiers have seen us, the night is quiet with only the moon giving off a faint light.

We somehow get to the wall and I squeeze Domino into the tight space. He moves calmly, letting me crouch between his legs. All I can do now is wait.

It seems forever until I finally hear rustling in the grass near me, my legs cramping as I stay as still as I possibly can in the tight space. I squint as I see shadows in the distance, relief floods over me as I make out Azure's silhouette, with the others following him, crouching near the trees. I'm just about to creep out when I see another movement near the building.

"Azure - help!" I cry out in my head, panicking.

Swiftly the snake turns and rises in an attack position. AJ, Alice, Peter and Anna freeze and turn around sensing the danger. We are all shocked to see Damian walking towards us. In the moonlight, I can just make out the smug expression he has on his face.

"I knew you were up to something!" He says, loud enough to draw attention from the soldiers. "All that time spent huddled together, then today, you all looked white and tense. I knew it!

Wait until the soldiers come, you'll all be killed for sure!"

"I'll tell them that you were a part of the plan," I say trying to sound confident, but my voice wavers with uncertainty. "Why else would you be here with us? Why didn't you tell a tutor instead? It's your word against all of ours."

"You little..." Damian says screwing up his face in concentration and a burst of pain enters my head so shocking I can no longer think. My body burns as I writhe in agony. Just then, a sound penetrates through its haze. It's singing, beautiful harmonious singing.

"Your body still
You cannot speak
No more chaos
Can you wreak."

There is a blinding light and the pain suddenly stops. There, standing on the grass with her arms pointing at Damian, is Dora. Damian is standing rigid unable to move. The singing was Dora, she has worked out her magic. She can freeze people like a statue.

"He's still alive," she says to me somewhat regretfully.

"Thank you," I tell her, getting to my feet.

"Is he dead?" Alice asks looking shocked.

"No, just frozen for a bit I think," I reply hesitantly.

"That's a shame," she whispers. "Now what are we going to

do? When he unfreezes, he's going to tell the tutors you were here and helped us escape." I look at everyone, panic consuming me.

"Peter... is there anything you can do? You can control minds... can you tell him not to speak?" I ask hysterically. Peter looks at me blankly then closes his eyes and frowns.

"I've done the best I can. He will remember Alice and AJ went out of the room but he didn't see you, Amelia. He went back to sleep and then thought all of this was a dream. I can't do anything more... Sorry," he apologises.

Damian seems to unfreeze and walks back towards the building, his eyes glazed and unblinking. All we can hope for now is that he isn't seen.

"Thank you so much, Peter," I say and look around. "You have to go... NOW!" I demand. Peter clambers onto Domino pulling AJ and Alice up behind him. They look down at me with a mixture of fear and excitement, as they cling on tightly. The horse shakes his head uneasily as AJ uses his magic, making them rise and glide smoothly over the wall. I watch anxiously as they disappear. Anna and I look at each other as we clasp hands breathing heavily. It's all up to them now to make sure the village is safe. We both creep back to the building, our eyes scanning for any movement.

"Stay where you are!" A commanding voice shouts behind us. We stop and I slowly turn around in horror. This is it - we have been found out; we are going to get shot!

"Oh, I'm sorry Mrs Steerly, I didn't realise it was you," the soldier says backing away slowly. Looking towards Anna, I gasp as she is no longer there! I try to hide a smile as I realise she has changed her appearance to Mrs Steerly.

"This girl came to tell me she heard a noise in the garden," Anna says, trying to put on the same cold, hard voice as the tutor. "Although I think it is just some stupid prank to get me out of bed. She will be punished. Go and finish checking whilst I see to her."

"Right away," the soldier says and hurries off towards the gardens.

I breathe a sigh of relief as we hurry as quietly but quickly as we can back up to our rooms. Relieved I see that Damian is in his bed asleep. I lay on my bed and sigh dramatically.

"Never let me do that again!" I say to Azure but I am asleep before I hear an answer.

Chapter 19

I wake with the sun shining through the window and a sudden feeling of guilt rushes over me. I can't believe I fell asleep when Peter, AJ and Alice are in danger. I feel so frustrated that there is no way to check they are alright or to know if they made it to the village.

Anna and I sit together at breakfast, trying to look relaxed and calm. We talk about our classes and how well we are getting on with our magic, trying to sound as normal as possible. Whilst we had to make the plan for the others to escape, Anna and I also had to make one for when we were left behind. This is going to be a difficult day, we just have to play our parts - our lives depend on it.

When the soldiers come and look for me in the garden just before Etiquette, it is no surprise when I am taken to Mrs Steerly's office. I take a deep breath and brace myself for what is to come as I follow the soldiers.

Anna is already seated in front of the desk looking white with fear but manages to give me a small reassuring smile. I'm relieved to see Mr Shielding standing nearby with Felix perched on his shoulder.

"Sit down," Mrs Steerly instructs. "Now that you are both

here, I would like to ask you a few questions."

I swallow and wipe my sweaty hands on my tunic, Anna and I don't have to act scared, this part is still very real. If we don't sound convincing, we could both be dead in a few hours.

"Have either of you seen or heard from James, Alice or Peter today?" Mrs Steerly asks.

"James?" Anna questions looking at me in confusion.

"AJ, his name is Arnold James," I reply. "The last time I saw Alice and AJ was last night when we all went to bed. When I got up, they were both gone. I saw Peter... a little bit earlier when I was talking to Anna in her room, " I say trying desperately to act confused and innocent.

"You didn't think them being gone was odd..." Mrs Steerly accuses.

"I thought that they had gone down to breakfast. I think I woke up a bit late." I reply shrugging like it was no big deal.

"But surely your friends not waking you is a bit unusual? They wouldn't have wanted you to miss breakfast, surely?" She asks.

"Alice, AJ and Peter are really good friends and Anna and I are good friends. Sometimes we all talk together as a group, but sometimes it is just Anna and me, the other three go off together sometimes." I say, shrugging again.

"I see," Mrs Steerly says taking a deep breath. "What about you, Anna. When did you last see your friends?"

Anna is twisting her tunic around her hands uncomfortably. She had confided in me that she wasn't good at lying, I hoped that she was better than she thought. As she replies her eyes pool with tears.

"They came into the room where Amelia and I were talking, then everyone left and we all went to bed. I didn't see Peter this morning," She says in a rush.

Mrs Steerly looks at us from one to the other. I can see she's considering whether to believe us or not. Her hard stare is difficult to read.

"Did they mention anything odd to you? Did they act strangely sometimes?" Mrs Steerly asks. Anna shakes her head quickly and looks down, I can see she's finding this very difficult. I start to panic, hoping that she doesn't admit to everything.

"They've spent a lot of time together recently... Anna and I feel a bit left out at times, especially as Alice and I were so close at the beginning, but we're still friends." I reply trying to sound a bit vague and I hadn't given it much thought.

"Very well," Mrs Steerly says and walks over to Mr Shielding, he hasn't said a word since I've been here. I can hear them talking quietly. We hoped that he would be here, Mrs Steerly will ask him if Felix thinks we are telling the truth. Mr Shielding will lie, then we should be in the clear. Just as I was about to breathe a sigh of relief thinking we had convinced Mrs Steerly there is a knock on the door and Damian barges in.

"I'm sorry to interrupt, Mrs Steerly but I have information about AJ and Alice," he says importantly. My heart starts to bang anxiously in my chest. What if Peter's mind control hasn't worked? What if Damian can remember what really happened? Mr Shielding looks confused and alarmed. Anna and I hadn't been able to tell him that we had been caught.

Mrs Steerly ushers Alice and I out of her office as fast as she can and slams the door behind us. We look at each other bleakly. We don't know what Damian is about to say. Will Mr Shielding be able to cover for us? We don't even know if our plan has worked at all.

Anna and I spend the rest of the day jumping at every unexpected movement. We try and spend as much time as we can on our own between classes, all that we can hear are conversations about Alice, AJ and Peter's disappearance and it is making us nervous.

"Do you think they made it?" Anna says to me anxiously. I shrug my shoulders. We can't possibly know.

I'm very worried as I go down to the stables for my lesson with Mr Shielding. Anna and I had been anxious all day about what Damian might have said. I had seen them both in class but the tutor had played his part well, never once looking at me and carrying on with the lesson as usual. Damian had ignored me and I had stayed as far away from him as possible. The lessons were very lonely without AJ and Alice and I felt miserable with worry.

When I go into the barn, Mr Shielding is standing in the

middle looking a little lost. We both look over at Domino's empty stall.

"Do they know he is missing as well?" I ask the tutor curiously.

"Yes, it does make us look a little suspicious. It would be very difficult to keep a horse quiet and calm trying to escape without our magic, but that couldn't be helped," he says. "Fortunately, Mrs Steerly trusts Felix and I. Damian says he only saw Alice and AJ leave the bedroom and that you were still in bed. He was a bit muddled after that, saying he saw everyone in the garden, but I managed to set it all straight. What happened when he saw you last night?"

I tell him about last night's events but when I come to Anna changing herself into Mrs Steerly, he stops me, looking worried.

"That could be a problem if the soldier is asked," Mr Shielding says thoughtfully. "Don't worry I will deal with it. We won't have your lesson today, you look exhausted."

I turn around and look at Domino's empty stall again, I miss him and hope that he is alright. Suddenly I spin around facing Mr Shielding again.

"Did it happen? Did they attack the village?" I ask guiltily, not believing I almost forgot to ask.

"Yes... they did but that's all I know," he says sadly. I wander sadly out of the barn and back up the lane. The broken door has been mended - just as though last night never happened.

Back in Anna's room, Azure and Anna's pixie, Lily, are

playing a game on Peter's bed. Lily has her back towards Azure and he is slithering towards her. Every time Lily looks around, Azure has to stop and pretend to be a statue. If Lily sees him move, then he's lost the game.

"We used to play that as kids," Anna says looking at them fondly.

Suddenly, there is a small 'pop' sound and on top of Tom's bed AJ's merturtle, Rio appears. Anna and I gasp in shock. Rio blinks rapidly and looks around, he sees me and smiles.

"What's happened? Is everyone OK?" I ask him out loud.

"We all got there safely," he says looking pleased. "The village was attacked. Your sister, Caroline is fine, but many others are hurt. Alice is doing all she can. Without the warning, it would've been a lot worse." Rio says, and then just as quickly as he appeared he vanishes once again. I relay the information that Rio has just told me.

"Phew... At least everyone is safe. Did he say why he left so quickly?" Anna asks.

"No, he said his little speech and then went," I say rather frustratedly. Anna and I sit in silence for a few minutes both thinking about what is happening in the villages.

"We can't let this carry on," Anna says determinedly. "Why is it illegal for the villagers to use their magic that the rich can use all of the time? Now the soldiers have attacked the village for no reason. Something has to change. If I don't become heir... If someone like Damian becomes heir, things are just going to get worse. We need to stop it now!"

"But how?" I ask. Anna is quiet for a few more minutes. I keep silent to let her think. Her eyes suddenly light up with excitement.

"AJ, Peter and Alice are out there with what I bet is a very upset village and we are in here, near the royals. If we can communicate to each other, we could all attack, we could start a rebellion," she announces looking wildly at me.

"Wait...How? We have no weapons... there are only other children here!" I exclaim. Anna rolls her eyes at me exasperated.

"Children and creatures that both have magic!" She cries. "Mr Shielding might be on board and some of the other tutors. Miss Clover seems pretty decent. My tutor, Mr Heartly might agree. We just need to figure it out, we just have to plan. If we know a way of getting out, then we also know a way of getting in! Most of the villagers have magic, if we can get them all in - then we can fight!"

Could we really take over the Royal Family, with all the soldiers protecting them? I shake my head in doubt. We can't do it... we'll all get killed. I look at Azure. If I hadn't been taken by the soldiers that day, then I would never have known him... Why should only the Royal Family get creatures, why should the wealthy only get to use magic? It's not fair and it's not right. At any time, Azure and I could be separated by them, rip us apart from each other just because they don't think we are worthy. I suddenly realise why Anna wants to become heir, we need change and becoming the heir seemed the only way, but now there is a glimmer of hope. We aren't going to do it by becoming royalty, by becoming one of them. We will do it by changing it together, by fighting for our freedom. My mind is made up.

"I'm in!" I shout excitedly.

Chapter 20

"What you are suggesting will be extremely dangerous with little chance of success!" Mr Shielding shouts frustratedly, waving his arms in the air. We are out in the fields far away from the building or any other children and tutors. I am riding another one of the horses, a nice brown girl. She's good but I still miss Domino. I have just told Mr Shielding the plan Anna and I came up with last night.

"But don't you see it will be better for everyone? Your plan of me becoming heir may change something eventually but the heir won't be in charge for twenty years at least. Change takes time. We want everyone to be able to have magic, everyone to be able to have a creature. This divide has to stop!" I shriek. "The villagers are angry and upset now! We know how to get them in to the castle grounds, we have people here to help. It's the perfect time!"

"I can understand how you feel," he says resigned. "But this isn't the way."

"Anna and I have to try. We will do it without your help," I say stubbornly. Mr Shielding looks at me and frowns.

"You remind me of your grandmother," he says huffily. "Fine, I'll help. Miss Clover probably will too but please be careful. When Rio comes back with another message tell him your idea, see if they can get the villagers on our side and then come straight to me!"

At breakfast the next morning everyone is shocked and alarmed When Mrs Steerly comes in and stands on the platform authoritatively. Everyone stops talking and looks at her, fear on their faces. Azure unwraps himself from around my wrist. He knows when Mrs Steerly is around nothing good happens, he's ready to strike if there's any sign of danger.

"Good morning, now we are lower on numbers you will all be invited to a special dinner... with the Royal Family!" She says beaming. "Remember your manners, remember your etiquette. I don't need to remind you what happens if you fail. The dinner will be in a week. Make sure you are all ready."

We all gasp in surprise; the room fills with mutterings and excited cries as Mrs Steerly leaves the room again.

"That would be the perfect time," Anna whispers to me. "The perfect time to strike." Realisation dawns on me. We are really doing this.

"How are we going to convince the other children to join in?" I ask Anna later that day whilst in the bedroom.

"They will all think as we do about their creatures, none will want to be parted from them," she explains. "Most come from the village, so if we can convince them that there was really an attack then they will probably agree. The rest... well, now they can use their magic they won't want to become a servant.

I think it will be fairly easy actually."

"But to fight... to possibly die...and for all of them to give up the hope of becoming heir? What about Damian and some of the others?" I ask doubtfully. "We are going to need all the help we can get; even from him!"

"We need to talk to everyone we can trust first and your job is also to talk to the creatures," she says.

"What? Why?" I ask confused.

"Because they are going to help to fight. They have to be warned what's about to happen. We need their help straight away, not just defending their owner," she says rather condescendingly.

"Who can we trust?" I ask. "I don't know anyone else."

"Well start talking to them then!" She replies. "Make friends and try to see how they felt about being taken away from their homes or if they actually want to be the next heir."

With my job set, I decide to start with the white group. I spend a lot of time with them in Mr Shielding's classes and now that AJ and Alice are gone there are only four of us left, Damian, Mia, Liam and me. Mia is a short girl with chestnut hair always in a plait. She looks younger than I am, but I know that she is 13 as she mentioned it was her birthday just after we first got here. She was sad that she wasn't with her family. She has a raven, which I could use to my advantage. He can read everyone's minds so questioning him could be useful to see who could be on my side. Liam is an older boy that always looks tired with messy hair, he doesn't do much in class except rest his head on the table and look out of the window vacantly. He is the one with a gargoyle. This is the only creature that I am not that comfortable speaking to. It has a large mouth with sinister-looking eyes and small horns on its head. Its wings curl around the side of its body, like a bat. I have seen it turn itself and other things into stone.

At the beginning of Business, I nervously go and sit next to Mia. She gives me an unsure look but then settles readying herself for the lesson.

"Is it OK if I sit here?" I ask her awkwardly. She nods and then faces forward. I try and think of other things to say but my brain just goes blank and I feel anxious.

"I like your raven. What's his name?" I ask pathetically.

"Her name is Skyla," she responds eyeing me with distrust. "Aren't you the one that's supposed to be able to talk to animals?"

"Yes..." I answer uncertainly.

"Then why didn't you just ask her yourself?" Mia asks nastily.

"I... I... I didn't want to be rude and talk to her without your permission," I say anxiously. Mia stares, assessing me.

"Thanks, that's actually quite decent of you," she says finally with a small smile. "Just don't listen to anything bad she says about me...otherwise I will have to tell you that she snores really badly, keeping Liam and I awake ALL night!" She laughs.

"I promise I won't," I say, joining in.

We talk a little more, I introduce her to Azure, and I pet Skyla but soon class starts and we concentrate on the lesson. However, Mia does whisper funny little comments here and there making me smother my laughter. Liam stares out of the window, looking bored.

"Do you two get on OK?" I ask Mia, tilting my head to Liam as we walk out of the class. Mia suggests going outside so we sit cross-legged in a sunny patch of grass. Skyla and Azure fly and slither around close by, like toddlers playing.

"Yeah... mostly," she says thoughtfully. "He doesn't say much. I think he's quite depressed actually. When Eddie, his gargoyle, hatched he got happier but now he's gone quieter again."

"That's a shame," I say sympathetically. "I don't get on well with Damian at all. It's better if we stay away from each other," I whisper.

"Why didn't you leave with the other's?" She asks curiously.

Everyone suspects that AJ, Alice and Peter escaped, even though Mrs Steerly tried to cover it up and said they were made into servants for not doing well enough. Anyone that knew Alice knew that she tried hard in every class, even asking questions and entering debates with the tutor. You only had to look at her and Dora to know that they had the strongest bond of any of us. There was no way that she had been removed.

I don't know what to say to Mia, I don't want to say anything that might ruin the small friendship that we have built. I decide that being honest is the only way for her to start to trust me. I look around hastily to see if anyone could be listening.

"They heard that there was an attack on the village, Alice can heal people so she went to see if she could help. AJ and Peter didn't want to be the heir," I answer.

Mia looks stunned "Oh no, is everyone OK? Why was there an attack?" She asks looking panicked.

"As far as we know most of the people are fine, AJ's merturtle can transport so he came back briefly and told us what was happening, but I don't know why they were attacked." Mia looks thoughtful and stays silent for a few minutes.

"So, you want to be the heir, that's why you stayed?" She asks.

"Anna and I want change," I say simply. It is then that I decide to talk to Skyla quickly, I ask her to read Mia's mind to see if I can trust her.

"Mia thinks that being taken was unfair, she misses her family and she is jealous that others got away and she didn't," is the bird's reply. I am overwhelmed with relief.

"I need to tell you something," I whisper. "But not here, come with me to my class with Mr Shielding, we can then all discuss it together."

Mia looks confused but nods. We change the subject to the weather until it is time for us to head to the stables.

When we meet up with Mr Shielding, I explain the plan of the rebellion to Mia. I also update the tutor on Anna's idea to start the attack when we are all having dinner with the Royal Family. Mia looks astounded but excited the more we talk.

"All the tutors will be at the meal and Miss Clover is with us on the plan," Mr Shielding states. "Mia, do you know anyone else that you can trust that you think will help? Remember, you are all risking your lives."

"Only Liam, I haven't talked to anyone in the red group," she replies sadly.

"No, I don't either, Damian hangs out with most of them," I say resigned. We end our conversation a while later and after the evening meal, I take Mia to Anna's room. Anna is very excited to see that we have another person join in the rebellion.

"Mia, take Amelia back to your room when Liam's there. Amelia, talk to the gargoyle, see what you can find out and then report back here." She says bossily.

Just then we hear a familiar 'pop'. AJ appears holding Rio's hand. Seeing Mia, AJ looks nervously around.

"Don't worry, she's OK!" I yell, hoping he won't disappear again. "Tell us everything!" I command. AJ looks relieved and gives Mia a small smile before sitting on the bed, eager to tell us what happened.

"Well, as you know the escape wasn't easy," AJ says, telling his side of the story. "Then Domino ran like the wind to the village. It was awful, we kept slipping and sliding on his back. I'm sure I was pulling his hair too hard most of the time. When we got there, we hid Domino in one of the farms, spreading black muck over all his white patches so no one recognised him. Then we eventually got to the market and all of us spread out to find our families. It was madness, people coming out of their houses at night and shouting at us. When they saw our creatures, things got even crazier. Some wanted to call for the soldiers but others believed us. We all went to the town hall... you know the one that hasn't got a roof? It was the only place that held enough people. We told them there was going to be an attack. We explained that we had been at the castle and why we had been taken against our will. People weren't happy about that at all. We told them to just be ready, if they were prepared and nothing happened then it would be no big deal, right? Alice then took me to your sister's house Amelia - she's fine. You don't need to worry. She kept asking us loads of questions about you and we told her as best we could. Really spirited that one though, kept begging us to take her here. Then the attack happened."

"How many were hurt? Was Alice able to heal them?" I ask worriedly. AJ shakes his head sadly.

"Some were killed. Mostly ones that hadn't believed us, unfortunately. A lot were injured, Alice helped as many as she could but her magic stopped working after a while. She had to keep resting. She felt so guilty about it. Dora zapped a few of the soldiers and we locked them up but still quite a lot of villagers were taken," he says sighing regretfully.

"How are they all now?" I ask him anxiously.

"Well, that's the thing, they are all acting crazy. They are gathering weapons; the blacksmith's wife was taken, so he is making any weapon he can. They are all wanting to storm the castle and rescue you all!" He finishes looking wide-eyed and panicked.

"That's great!" Anna screams enthusiastically.

We proceed to tell AJ the plan, that in a few days we will all be in the castle for the dinner with the Royal Family. That's when we will attack. AJ looks at us as though we have all gone mad but promises to spread the word at the village. I give him a big hug before he disappears along with Rio.

That evening Azure and I head back to my room feeling optimistic. We might be able to do this if we can just get the others on our side. We walk in and Azure heads to the tank and then stops dead, just before plopping in.

"This smells funny," he says confused.

"Maybe it needs to be cleaned out?" I suggest. Azure refuses to sleep in it so I reluctantly head down to Miss Clovers office and knock on her door.

"Come in!" She shouts in her usual cheery voice. I haven't seen Miss Clover other than in passing for a while as I now take most of my classes with Mr Shielding. I find that I have missed her friendly manner.

"Azure won't go in the tank, we think it's dirty," I say, a little exasperated at Azure's stubbornness. I mean how much dirtier did it get in one night? He slept in it fine before.

"Oh... Ok, I will see to it tomorrow," she says looking concerned. "I have a bowl he can use for tonight." Handing me a fishbowl. I mutter my thanks and head upstairs, washing the bowl in the bathroom and filling it with water. I place the bowl by my bed and Azure slips into it contentedly.

It is still dark when I hear Damian screaming fiercely, the sound so loud I have to cover my ears.

"What is it?" I shout at him as I watch him curl up into a ball and sob. Damian doesn't say anything as he holds his head in his hands and cries. I don't feel comfortable watching him, even though Damian is nasty, spiteful and smug, looking at how vulnerable and upset he is, is disturbing.

After a few moments, more children come into the room asking what the matter is. I shrug helplessly. A tall boy from the red group comes further into the room and looks at the tank.

"Oh no!" He exclaims pointing at Melvin, Damian's merturtle. I look over and see Melvin at the top of the tank. He is floating upside down lifelessly. I gasp out loud, shocked.

"What did you do?" The boy demands looking at me.

"I didn't do it!" I shout innocently.

"Yeah, right!" He says and comes towards me, backing me into a corner. Azure slithers in front of me, raising his head, poised to attack.

"If I had done it, don't you think Damian would be blasting my brain out?" I yell trying to make them see sense. The boy stops and looks around uncertainly.

"I did it, I did it, I didn't mean to," Damian mumbles in the corner and starts to rock back and forth.

We are then fortunately interrupted by Miss Clover who quickly assesses the situation and sends everyone back to bed. She takes hold of Damian in one hand and Melvin in the other and walks out of the room.

"Are you OK?" Anna asks softly and sits on my bed with Mia beside her. Azure slithers up to the door, appearing to be on guard.

"I have no idea," I say, shocked and confused.

"I'll stay with you tonight," Anna says and gets into Alice's bed, her pixie by her side.

"I will too," says Mia and gets in another one, Skyla resting on her hair as though it were a nest.

"Thank you," I mumble and slip under my covers.

Just as I am about to give up any hope of sleeping, I feel Azure curl up beside me. I sigh as I relax properly for the first time since I had been woken, his body feels reassuring next to me. I close my eyes contentedly and drift off to sleep.

Chapter 21

The next day we all wait anxiously as Mrs Steerly climbs determinedly onto the platform; her face grim.

"Damian has committed a serious crime. He has taken the life of his creature. As you all know, the punishment for such a crime is death. It will be carried out tomorrow morning," she says looking disturbed. I look at Anna and Mia sitting opposite me.

"Why would Damian do such a thing?" I ask confused.

They both look cluelessly at each other, then Anna looks at me thoughtfully.

"Where was Azure sleeping last night? He wasn't in the tank," she asks suspiciously. I explain about Azure refusing to enter the water and having to go and get another bowl from Miss Clovers.

"The tank must have had some sort of poison in it then... but Damian was saying he did it. That he didn't mean it. Did he mean for Azure to sleep in it?" She says, sounding shocked.

"Oh no!" gasps Mia covering her face with her hands.

"You don't mean he tried to kill Azure, do you?" I ask bewildered. Anna just nods. I think of Damian for a few minutes. Even though he is an awful person he doesn't deserve to die

- does he?

"We have to save him," I say quietly, leaning forward over the table. They both look at me like I have gone mad, their mouths open in astonishment.

"We need him for the attack. We need all the help we can get and his magical ability is useful," I tell them earnestly. Anna, looking thoughtful explains to Mia that Damian can cause people pain. Mia looks shocked.

"So... what's the plan then?" She asks excitedly. We all look at each other cluelessly, each hoping for an idea.

By lunch, Anna has thought of a plan but it doesn't sound easy at all. It also means getting some more help, which is the reason why Anna, Mia and I are all outside the red rooms door knocking loudly. After a gruff sounding 'come in' we all open the door and go inside.

"What do you want?" A tall boy with large muscles and short cropped hair says as we enter. I remember this is Andrew, he got an award along with Anna and Damian. Fortunately, he is the one we came to speak to and the only one in the room. I close the door as Anna glides towards him, not looking at all nervous - not at all like Mia and me. She stands in front of him and smiles sweetly.

"You can go invisible, can't you?" She says innocently. Andrew's eyes screw up spitefully as he stares down at her.

"Yeah... and?" He says cockily.

"You liked Damian, didn't you? You were friends? What if

I told you we could get him out safely?" She says, matching his tone. I can see Andrew's jaw tense as he considers how to answer. He looks at us all trying to assess the situation. He glances at Azure distrustfully.

"I'm listening," he says finally, sitting on his bed. Mia and I stand quietly as Anna explains the plan, hardly daring to breathe and wishing we had Andrew's ability to become invisible.

"But if we do this, you must do as we say when the time comes? Got it, that's the deal?" Anna says as she finishes. Back in the village, making deals was like a bond between people. We took them seriously and they were never broken. So as Andrew nods his head, we know that he is on our side. Next, we head to Mia's room where we all barge in. Liam looks a little shocked to find the room full with all of us standing in front of him.

"We need a little talk," says Mia, looking happy once again. "We need to... borrow Eddie, your gargoyle, tonight," she says smiling.

"Why?" Liam asks suspiciously.

It wasn't part of our plan that we tell him about the dinner and rebellion just yet but I figure he has to know some time, so we might as well do it now. So, I tell him everything, finishing with why we need to rescue Damian.

"OK, I'm in," he says shrugging and points to Eddie sitting on the floor beside the bed. Eddie has turned himself to stone.

"He'll be like that until dark. That's how he rests."

We all gather back at my room and go over the plan once again. Whilst we had been gone, Skyla, Mia's raven had been out on a mission - to find out exactly where Damian was being held. Skyla reports to me and I tell the group.

"It's where we expected. He's down in the jail, with two soldiers outside." We all take a deep breath; everything is in place. Now we just have to do it!

Chapter 22

Just the same as the night of the escape we all pretend to be asleep for when the tutors come and check on us. After this, we all gather in my room for a last-minute check.

"Does everyone know what they have to do?" I say to Anna, Mia, Andrew, Azure, Skyla and Eddie.

"Yes!" they all chorus together. We all creep down as close to the jail as we can get, trying to keep to the shadows and out of sight. Azure wraps himself around Andrew's wrist and Eddie sits on his shoulder. I have given the animals their instructions. Hopefully, they know exactly what to do.

Andrew gives a tight blink then all three of them disappear. We can hear soft footsteps go down the hall. We wait a few moments in silence.

"Right, now it's your turn," I say to Anna. She looks worriedly at us. She has never tried to use her magic for such a long time, this will be a challenge. Her face distorts and changes until it merges into Mrs Steerly. We watch as she rushes down the corridor while Mia and I creep into one of the rooms.

"Is this going to work?" Mia asks me worriedly.

"It should do if it all goes to plan," I say trying to sound convincingly. "Right now, Andrew should be invisible at the jail, ready for our diversion. Anna, whilst being Mrs Steerly, will tell the soldiers to go check what's happening whilst she stays and guards the jail. Andrew and Azure will open the prison door, using Azure's super strength. They will then get Damian out with Eddie making a Damian shaped statue in his place. We then get Damian over the wall and out to freedom with hopefully a promise from him to help the rebellion."

Mia doesn't look convinced, but she doesn't say anything. Guessing that it's about time for our part of the plan I nudge Mia. Using her magic, she sets fire to a piece of paper and lets it land on some books. We run down the corridor as quietly as we can and hide behind a bend in the wall.

"Can I smell smoke?" Anna asks the soldiers, as she sniffs the air.

The soldiers look at each other in panic and race off down the corridor. Hurriedly we race past her and head towards one of the doors near the kitchen, a door Mr Shielding said he would leave open for us. After a few torturous minutes, Andrew and Damian join us with the creatures.

"All gone to plan so far?" I say in a rush.

Andrew nods and hands over Azure and Damian. He is going to drop Eddie back with Liam and then he's going to go back to his room. His job is done.

"Come on Damian!" I whisper as loud as I can. We run to the wall, trying to keep to the shadows. "You will meet the villagers for the attack, won't you?" I ask sternly.

"Yes, I understand the deal Andrew told me," he says in his usual arrogant tone. "Was this really your idea to save me?" He asks uncertainly. I give him a hard look.

"Yes," I say crossly. "You've been horrible from the start and you nearly killed Azure... but you paid for that, I'm guessing. Now you can help us take back the kingdom. Your magic is amazing, you will be a great help." I'm not sure but I think I see a blush spread into Damian's cheeks. It could just be the light though or the effort of running.

When we get to the wall, I get Mia and Damian to work together to push me high enough so I can clamber up to the top. It is very uneven and hard to balance but I crouch trying to steady myself, using Azure as a rope Damian pulls himself up to join me at the top.

"Thank you," Damian says as he attempts to scramble down the wall then jumps the rest of the way before landing clumsily on the grass below. He puts his thumb up, grinning before he runs off into the darkness. I watch him, envious of his freedom. With the others help, I struggle back down wishing it wasn't so high as I graze my stomach on the rough wall. Mia and I run back inside and up to Anna's room as quietly as we can, exhausted. We don't have to wait long before Anna joins us. She lays on the bed looking drained.

"Did it work?" I whisper harshly.

"Yes, I think so." Anna says giving a big sigh "There were times when my magic wobbled but I don't think they noticed.

I'm just going to sleep for a few weeks now." We all head back to our rooms exhausted. Hoping that it was a job well done.

Chapter 23

It doesn't take long for the news of Mia, Anna, Andrew and I saving Damian to go around the other children, and they all congratulate us quietly. We all feel proud of ourselves, we knew it was the right thing to do. Andrew convinces the others to be on our side and to fight for our rebellion, this was the deal we made with him, but I secretly think that he would have done it anyway. He is not a fan of the royals.

With their owner's permission, I instruct all of the creatures on what they should do and what to expect. None of them want to be separated from their owners that they are bonded with and will happily fight for the chance to stay with them. They don't show any fear or nervousness about the task ahead.

To my delight, the night before the Royal dinner, Rio transports Alice to my bedroom. She looks tired and anxious, but something is different about her, she looks more confident than when she left, her eyes shining with determination. We hug tightly for a long time before we tell each other our news. The village is eager and ready for the rebellion and Damian is with them.

"Your sister talks about you constantly. When I went to see her, she didn't stop asking me questions. She's amazed at your magical abilities," she says to me before she leaves.

"Tell her I miss her," I say, then with a 'pop' Alice is gone. I wanted to say more, to tell my sister that I love her, that I hoped after this we could fix our relationship, but I didn't want her to hear it from Alice. I want to be able to tell her face to face.

I feel sad and scared as I sit on my bed with Azure in his tank. We may all die tomorrow, Alice or Anna may be killed. Villagers may die. We are risking so much for the hope of change, so much for our freedom to be who we are meant to be. I just hope that it is worth it.

The morning of the Royal dinner comes and Mrs Steerly gives us strict instructions of what to expect. I don't know whether I should feel nervous, excited or terrified and glancing around I see the same expressions flitting across the other's faces. We pass the morning lessons in a daze. After these are finished, we are expected to get cleaned up and looking our best in the special clothes we have been given to wear.

"Why do we have to wear a dress?" Mia complains, pushing her arms through the sleeves. "I've never worn one in my life!"

"I rather like them, they make me feel quite pretty," Anna says, looking into a mirror, a blush rising in her cheeks.

I look at mine in disgust. Mia's is blue, Anna's is red but mine is a horrible mustard colour. Each of them has flowers sewn into them and netting under the skirt.

"At least yours are nice colours," I say looking at theirs in envy. "Mine looks like old straw." We are all getting ready in my room, which the others have been sleeping in with me, using the other beds that were unoccupied.

"It's time to go!" Andrew bursts in shouting. He then stops and looks at Anna, his mouth hanging open. He then shakes his head a little and clears his throat. "Come on!" Anna turns an even darker shade of pink and follows after him, looking smug.

Carrying our creatures, we walk towards the castle. This is the first time we have seen it as the buildings we have been living in have shielded it from view. As we get closer, I look up at the dark stone, the towers look so tall that they could reach the clouds. It is huge, much bigger than I could ever have imagined. Everyone is quiet, giving each other nervous glances. I look enviously at Anna walking beside me in her beautiful gown, the image of a confident princess. I try hard not to trip in my dress as I hold tightly to Mia's hand.

As the large double doors are opened for us to enter, we see the brilliance of the decor inside. There's a thick red carpet running down the centre with white pillars evenly spaced on either side. There are chandeliers of gold, suits of armour and paintings so large that they are as tall as my house back home.

We continue to be silent, with our mouths open in astonishment as we follow Mrs Steerly from room to room, each one grander than the one before. Mr Shielding walks soberly next to me. Over the past few days, we haven't talked very much except about the plan and trying to increase Azure's magic. I miss our little conversations as we got to know one another, he doesn't feel like one of the tutors, more like a friend.

"Are you sure you want to do this? There's still time to back out," Mr Shielding whispers to me urgently.

I briefly think about his words, for all of us to go back and live life how we have been for the past few weeks. For more of us to leave to become servants, for more mistakes to be made and lives to be taken. I just can't do it. I won't. I nod my head as I look into his eyes trying to show him that I am determined, that all of us deserve better than how we have been living.

We reach what I assume is the dining hall. The walls are dark red with golden railings. Looking up there is a painting on the ceiling of dragons in battle. In the middle of the room, white flowers are arranged on a huge circular table with gold cutlery and plates set around them. There are two large throne-like chairs that must be for the King and Queen, apart from these we can sit where we like. I choose a chair between Mia and Anna. The tutors are interspaced between us and I'm happy to see Mr Shielding is a few seats away from me.

"This is amazing!" Anna whispers. "The best birthday meal I'm ever going to get I think," she says to me in wonder.

"Congratulations!" I exclaim as quietly as I can. "How old are you?"

"I'm sixteen," she replies.

I take a deep breath and try to steady my nerves. We are starting a rebellion on Anna's birthday. She may not live to see the end of it, or she could be captured and sent to be a servant. For a moment I panic and look around wildly. Maybe we should stop this? Maybe there is another way? But none of us has practised a signal for if any of us wants to back out. It has to happen; there's no stopping it! My thoughts are interrupted by two servants entering through a side door, carrying a large box, which appears to be made of glass.

"Could all creatures enter the box, please?" One says loudly.

We all look at each other in confusion. No, no, no. We need them. How are we going to be able to defeat the royals without our creatures? This is a disaster! My heart starts to beat wildly in my chest as I look at the box frustratedly.

"Don't worry, we will find a way out," Azure reassures me as he slithers into the box. The other creatures all follow meekly. The lock is turned, and they all look sadly out, some pressing their hands to the glass.

All the other children look towards me, panic clear in their eyes, searching mine for instructions. I try to nod reassuringly as I desperately think of something that will work to free the creatures. There must be some way! My thoughts are interrupted by loud trumpeting filling the air and the King and Queen are announced. We all stand, waiting for them to take their places at the table.

Nothing could have prepared me for the sight of their entrance. The Queen looks at each of us, disdain marring her severe features. Her hair is perfectly coiled at the base of her neck, and long gold earrings are hanging from her lobes. The King has a friendlier face, but his eyes are haunted with sadness. Their clothes are layers of gold and red looking majestic and expensive but what shocks me the most are the large dragons perched on each of their shoulders.

The Queen's dragon is blue with green scales on its chest and tail while the King's is varying shades of grey and black. Both have evil, slitted eyes and fierce expressions.

I almost forget to bob into a small curtsy as the royal's enter, so entranced I am by the dragons. Fortunately, I remember just in time, a little behind the others. The King and Queen sit and then with a tilt of the Queen's head she allows us to be seated.

The room is suddenly filled with servants entering the room, looking tired and sickly. Their grey faces are pinched and their eyes lifeless and glazed. They each place a bowl of soup in front of us and leave quickly. I think I see a familiar face amongst them, someone I once knew back at the village, but I am not certain. The Queen gracefully picks up her spoon and sips elegantly. We all copy her, trying to behave appropriately.

It could be the best soup in the world, but I feel too sick to eat it. All this time we have been planning, working hard, getting us all together, communicating with the villagers. It has all come to this moment. We need our creatures; without them, we have no hope of winning. We cannot progress with the rebellion; I feel so hopeless!

The Queen starts to talk to some of the other children, who

nervously answer. She asks about where they grew up, if they knew they had magic, what magic they have and now what magic their creatures have. The King looks absently into his bowl.

"Eugh, this is boring!" A voice says near the Queen. I look up startled, someone would be shot for saying that out loud. Slowly I realise that it is the Queen's dragon, perched on the back of the throne. She is talking to me. I am suddenly filled with relief as an idea forms in my mind.

"Would you like to liven it up a bit?" I ask mischievously.

"How?" She asks curiously. With a calculating look on her face.

"Get the creatures out!" I command.

I have been wondering about this for a while but haven't put it to the test yet. At first, I just thought it was a coincidence, that I could not only talk to the creatures and animals but that I could also order them what to do. It all started with AJ's egg, why did it hatch just because I asked it to? Why did Felix do a loop even though it was uncomfortable for him? When Damian's merturtle slapped him because I wished it. They all seemed to obey, no matter what I asked. I was, however, taking a very big risk now. This was the Queen's dragon and if it so wished could set fire to the room in a second, but it just looks at me and blinks its eyes. Suddenly, it unfurls its wings and flaps them loudly. Everyone stops the conversation as they look at the dragon, shock on their faces. The dragon dives towards the box and picks it up with its talons and rises into the air. She flies with it across the room until she is hovering over the table. It is then that she releases it, smashing the glass and breaking the table. The creatures climb out of the cube, some are covered in blood, but I have no time to think about it now. I have started it; the attack must happen now.

"Attack the King and Queen," I command to the dragons. I watch as they obey, jets of fire whooshing out of their mouths as they hit the royals. I look into the Queen's eyes, panic and disbelief are the last thing I see before she is engulfed in flames and both the King and Queen fall to the floor. Soldiers race into the room from all around and the room is in chaos.

"Azure, come to me!" I command and look around. Miss Clover is picking up chairs using her magic and throwing them at the soldiers. I think Andrew has gone invisible as I see a soldier fall to the ground with apparently no attack. Mia is setting fire to anything that comes near her. All around me there is fighting, magic bursting from every child and creature. Anna grabs hold of me and I turn to her in shock.

"It's time to go!" She shouts.

I command the dragons to follow me as we rush out of the room and back out of the castle. Soldiers are spilling out of rooms and running towards the dining room. Anna merges and changes her face to a soldier and grabs me tightly. If anyone should look at us, they would hopefully think that I was captured and being taken away. The dragons flying overhead don't help this illusion though.

In my head, I am devastated to hear the dragon's cry. They are mourning the loss of their owners, guilt wracking their bodies and minds. I try and tell them it's for the best but they will not listen, following my orders despite their grief.

We finally get to the wall. I take a deep breath, I am suddenly very anxious as everything depends on me completing the next task.

"This is it, Azure, I hope you are ready," I tell him.

This is what we have been practising for. Azure holds on to me tightly as I place my hands against the stone. The snake glows the brightest blue I have ever seen him, his hiss so loud that it hurts my ears. I feel the stones budge slowly under my palms, moving and sliding but it isn't enough. I start to scream in agony, as my arms burst in pain and the flesh on my hands is ripped open. It is still not enough.

"Help me!" I cry out in agony.

Anna feebly pushes with her arms, not making any difference. It is then that I hear the flap of wings. I had forgotten they were there but my command was heard. The two dragons help to push the wall. At first, I think that it still isn't enough, that the wall was much stronger than we first thought but with a sudden jerk, it collapses and we all fall forward into the rubble.

I look up and see rows and rows of faces. The whole village is armed and they look angry and determined. I don't even have time to get up before they are all rushing through the hole we've created. Before I am trampled on, there is a hand reaching out to me, it is Damian's.

"Come on, otherwise we are going to miss all the fun!" He tells me cheekily. He gets me back on my feet and rushes off. Everyone races past me heading for the castle, Azure is still firmly on my arm and the two dragons are gliding back up in the air.

"Don't hurt any of the villagers!" I tell the dragons then get them to follow me once again. I want to find Alice and AJ, but looking for them would take too much time, we all need to get back to the castle, to fight the soldiers. The entrance is swarming with people, turmoil is everywhere, but as I run to join in, I trip, my hands slam onto the ground painfully and I look at what I have fallen over. Miss Clover is laying on the floor, her eyes open and vacant. I gasp in shock and horror and scoot over to the wall. I try and breathe in and out slowly but my heart is beating too fast and my lungs are burning. I can't breathe. I look around me for help, my eyes darting from person to person frantically. I must find Alice, Alice can save Miss Clover, all she has to do is use her magic. Further down the hall, I see a little blue creature zapping soldier after soldier, making them freeze - It's Dora! I quickly scramble up, trying to dodge out of everyone's way but a soldier runs towards me. Azure springs off my arm hissing fiercely, his fangs bared. With the soldier distracted I run towards the nymph. Surely Alice is nearby? I look around frantically, but I don't see her.

"Dora!" I cry out desperately, "Where is Alice?" Dora looks towards me and that's when I look behind her in horror, Mrs Steerly grabs Dora and places her hand over her head. I watch as Dora's life leaves her body.

At first, I think the ear-piercing shriek comes from me, but I realise it is Alice as she comes barging through the crowd of people. She looks between Dora and Mrs Steely and rushes to her creature, her hands glowing brightly.

I don't know if I order it or not, but I look on stunned as the dragons appear over our heads breathing fire. I stare boldly at Mrs Steerly as she looks above us in horror, having the same fate as the royals. I did not wish to kill her. My aim was only the Royal Family, to bring change to the kingdom. As I look at Mrs Steerly's burnt remains my mind shuts down at the horror of what I have just done. I watch Alice's desperation as she tries to revive Dora, I look around at the other bodies littering the floor, some soldiers, some children. Their eyes staring lifelessly to the ceiling, their bodies broken. What have I just done? I close my eyes as my knees collapse from under me as I fall to the floor.

Chapter 24

I don't know how much time passes until I open my eyes to that familiar white room, the one I had woken in a few weeks ago. My vision is blurry as I look around at people and creatures in beds, sitting and standing around. Bandages wrapped around hands, arms and legs. Azure is curled up beside me but lifts his head as he senses I'm awake.

"Are you OK?" I ask him.

"Yes, a bit tired still, how are you?" He asks me.

"I'm OK, I think," I reply.

I look around the room, trying to see anyone I recognise. I see Andrew and Liam and a few villagers I know from home. A wave of sadness washes over me as I see the tears in their eyes and the tiredness of their faces.

"Did we...Did we win?" I ask Azure tentatively.

"Yes, we won," he sighs happily. I expect to feel elated; we have done what we set out to do! This is a victory but all I feel is numb. A wariness fills my body and mind.

Azure wraps himself around my wrist and I get up to walk around the room. I see Alice looking tired and pale sitting next to a man's bed, her fingers glowing. I suddenly remember what I saw happen to Dora. Terrified I look around hurriedly but don't see her anywhere. I pause where I'm standing. I want to go up to Alice to make sure she's OK, to see if Dora is alright but I'm scared. Alice loved her nymph so much; their bond was so strong that I don't know how she will cope without her. I take a deep breath and head towards her, if Dora is dead then I will help Alice the best I can. I may not have the magic to heal her, but I can be with her as a friend should be.

Alice looks up as I come towards her, her eyes are glossy and red. I reach out and hug her tightly. We don't need words; we have been through so much together. Fighting for survival in the village, being taken, when I found out I had magic, the lessons, the plans. Everything goes through my head.

"Is Dora...?" I ask not being able to finish. Am I asking if she is alive or dead? More tears well up in her eyes and she blinks, a single tear rolling down her face.

"She's OK... I managed to save her... She's OK," she says relieved. I smile broadly at her and realise my cheeks are also wet with tears. I didn't think she would be; I didn't believe that even Alice could save her; I was wrong. I give her another small squeeze and then let her carry on trying to heal the many wounded.

I don't know where I'm headed as I walk through the corridors, being back in the building where they had kept us for the past few weeks feels strange. When I first got here, I was scared and worried as I didn't have any magic, but I have found out a lot about myself here. It now feels like a home to me even though there was so much anxiety and panic. I reach the stables and head inside. I'm not surprised when I see Mr Shielding, I think that I expected him here, he was the reason I came.

"Oh, there you are Amelia!" He says smiling widely. "I'm very relieved to see you!"

"I'm glad to see you're OK too," I say sadly, thinking back to seeing Miss Clover's body on the floor.

"So, you know then? She was a great person; I wish you could've known her better," he says regretfully.

"Does Felix tell you everything that goes in my head?" I ask feeling a bit annoyed. I suddenly think of something that I have been meaning to ask for a while.

"How do you have Felix? I thought only the Royal Family can have creatures?" I ask him curiously.

"Ah!" He says perking up slightly. "I wondered when you were going to ask. I am the Queen's... I mean Harriet's brother. Therefore, I was a part of the Royal Family and so could have a creature." I look at him in horror. I made him go along with a plan to stop the royals and I killed his sister and her husband!

"I am so sorry," I apologise but no words seem good enough.

"She was my sister and I loved her," he says with tears in his eyes. "But they were all bad people and they were getting worse, her son Austin was the cruellest boy you could've imagined. That's why I killed him." At first, I think I must have heard him wrong and look at him in confusion.

"I have a confession," he says looking at me sadly. "I ordered his creature to kill him – the same way that you killed his parents. His ideas for the village were beyond evil, I couldn't let him become King and carry them out. After he was... gone I persuaded the royals to take you and the other children around your age to become the next heir, it was a risk I had to take because you, Amelia, are my granddaughter. You are the rightful heir."

I look at him in shock. This man that was my tutor, he had become someone I trusted and had involved with many of my plans, who had taught me so much about myself and my magic - he is my grandfather?

"How?" I demand.

"I used to sneak out, as I told you, remember?" He replies. "I met your grandmother and we fell in love and your mother was born. I came to see her as much as I could. She knew the truth about me, but then my sister found out and I was banned from going back to the village. Harriet said that she would kill me and everyone I loved if I left. It broke my heart."

My mind buzzes with information. I don't know who is going to become the new ruler of the kingdom. We hadn't discussed it, we thought that the adults would choose someone... Will they still do that? Or will they continue with the royal line? Could I become the next queen? My mind is swirling chaotically. "I have to go and think..." I say feebly as I stumble out of the stable for the last time.

Chapter 25

It takes a long time for the decision to be made about who is to lead the kingdom. My name is mentioned many times and I am forced to attend meetings and discussions. I accept in front of a mixture of villagers and nobles that I am the heir, but I refuse to take a throne. I nominate Anna.

"Why do you want me to run your kingdom?" She asks me shocked, after I give her the news.

"Because you realised we needed to change, and you gave us the courage to fight for it. That is what makes a good ruler. And anyway... I hate it all, it's all mind-numbingly boring!" I say to her and we both laugh. I feel confident that Anna will do the best she can. She could always see the good things that being a royal could accomplish and she was brave and determined to make sure it happened.

I'm in the tiny, one-roomed house that I grew up in when the announcement is called that Anna will become the next ruler. She won't be a queen as we have abolished royalty. Everyone can now use magic and have a creature; it is how we all planned and what we fought for. Mr Shielding, my grandfather, helps her in any way that he can and I go and visit them often; I am always welcome. The castle is now mainly used for the homeless with Anna choosing to live in a house nearby.

I sigh as I look around my home. Everything is so familiar here but it is so quiet. I miss the children and creatures talking around me. I realise that my life can never be the same as it was before. If I went back to work on the farms it would be tarnished by Tom's absence. The Blacksmith was killed in the fight, so I no longer have a job there. I don't know what to do with my life now. My sombre thoughts are interrupted by the door banging open.

"I have it, I have it!" Caroline shouts excitedly as she rushes inside with something wrapped tightly in her arms. Alice follows behind beaming brightly, Dora sitting crossed-legged on her shoulder. Caroline puts the wrapped object gently on the bed. She smiles at me brightly, her dimples showing. Tears spring to my eyes as I am overwhelmed with happiness. I may not know where my life is headed but the bond between my sister and I has been fixed. There is nowhere else I would rather be than with her.

"I've come to tell you the good news!" Alice says excitedly to me. "You are to be in charge of breeding and looking after the creatures. They are in high demand! There's no one better qualified!" I open and shut my mouth, too shocked to say anything. Alice abruptly turns and looks at the object. "Hurry up! I need to see!" Alice complains crouching near the bed where Caroline is carefully unwrapping it.

I come and stand between them and look at the package curiously. There, covered in phoenix feathers is an egg; Caroline's egg and it has swirls of red.

"Looks like you are going to have a fiery playmate!" I tease Azure happily. He hisses, slithers off my wrist towards his tank and hides under a rock.

Thank you for reading!

If you enjoyed Magic and Me, please leave a review on Amazon - I love reading them! You can also find details of my other books on Amazon too.

If you would like to follow me on Instagram, or email me and go on my mailing list, I will keep you updated of any new releases and news.

Instagram – julia_hall_childrens_author

Email – juliahall690@gmail.com

Turn over the page to see how Amelia's adventure continues in…

Magic and Me 2 – Magic, Me, and the Golden Egg

Coming soon on Amazon

Magic and Me 2 – Magic, Me, and the Golden Egg

After fighting for their freedom, Amelia is content breeding magical creatures - until disease spreads through the eggs, destroying any hope of trading them for the precious supplies they need.

Desperate to help her people before everything is ruined, Amelia and her friends search for something that can save them all - a mysterious *golden* egg!

What could be inside it?

Amelia soon realises that having magic is still as dangerous as it was before the rebellion, but now there is a different enemy to fight...

About the author

Julia lives in Bristol with her husband and 3 children. She's loved books from a young age and would always spend her pocket money on buying more!

Now she has a house full of books ~ much to her husband's dismay but she tries to only keep her favourites.

As well as writing and reading she loves walking her dogs and playing computer games with her children.

Acknowledgements

A very special thank you to my mum who I spent many hours talking on the phone with. Sorry I made you read the story so many times and helping me edit at 4 am!

To my daughter who sat by my side and patiently listened to my ideas. To all the rest of my family for supporting and helping me to make my dream come true.

To the whole of the 'Bear with us' team. Andy and your super fast emails. Leanne and Luisa, the cover is brilliant and captures the magic perfectly ~ I am amazed by your talents!

Thank you so much for creating the story I envisioned.

Printed in Great Britain
by Amazon